GIRLS AGAINST GOD

GIRLS AGAINST GOD

Translated
by Marjam Idriss

VERSO
London • New York

NORLA
NORWEGIAN LITERATURE ABROAD

This translation has been published with the financial support of NORLA

This English-language edition first published by Verso 2020
First published as Å hate Gud © Forlaget Oktober 2018
Translation © Marjam Idriss 2020

The publisher and author would like to thank the following for quotations appearing in the text: Darkthrone mini-documentary, bonus material from the CD compilation *Preparing for War* (2000); Heinrich Kramer and James Sprenger (translated by Montague Summers), *Malleus Mallificarum* (1928); Darkthrone, 'Over Fjell Og Gjennom Torner', *Transylvanian Hunger* (1994).

5 7 9 10 8 6

Verso
UK: 6 Meard Street, London W1F 0EG
US: 20 Jay Street, Suite 1010, Brooklyn, NY 11201
versobooks.com

Verso is the imprint of New Left Books

ISBN-13: 978-1-78873-895-8
ISBN-13: 978-1-78873-897-2 (US EBK)
ISBN-13: 978-1-78873-896-5 (UK EBK)

British Library Cataloguing in Publication Data
A catalogue record for this book is available from the British Library

Library of Congress Cataloging-in-Publication Data

Names: Hval, Jenny, 1980– author. | Idriss, Marjam, translator.
Title: Girls against God / [Jenny Hval] ; translated by Marjam Idriss.
Other titles: Å hate Gud. English
Description: English language edition. | London ; New York : Verso, 2020. |
   Summary: "Jenny Hval's second novel in English is a radical fusion of feminist thought and experimental horror, and a unique treatise on magic, writing, and art."— Provided by publisher.
Identifiers: LCCN 2020016886 (print) | LCCN 2020016887 (ebook) | ISBN 9781788738958 (paperback) | ISBN 9781788738972 (ebk)
Classification: LCC PT8952.18.V35 A7413 2020 (print) | LCC PT8952.18.V35 (ebook) | DDC 839.823/8--dc23
LC record available at https://lccn.loc.gov/2020016886
LC ebook record available at https://lccn.loc.gov/2020016887

Typeset in Electra by Biblichor Ltd, Edinburgh
Printed and bound by CPI Group (UK) Ltd, Croydon CR0 4YY

Girls Against God

A NOVEL

Jenny Hval

1

THE WITCHCRAFT

It's 1990, and I'm the Gloomiest Child Queen.

I hate God.

It feels primitive and pitiful to say it, but I'm a primitive and pitiful person.

The screen in front of me shows images from 1990: images of pine trees; the tops, grey sky. The video flickers and the camera sways across a pixelated digital universe. A boy, possibly Nocturno Culto, walks through the forest to the sound of brutal guitar riffs. The camera lens follows him lazily. The image jerks at each footstep as the camera operator tramples the boy's trail. Is this a kind of genesis? In my film notes I jot down: 'Home video, in line with the lo-fi aesthetic of the genre. Short, enigmatic and ugly video riffs on details from boring Norwegian landscape.'

I also note: 'I hate God.' What a smug thing to say, but I'm pretty smug. (Isn't 'me' just a different word for 'God'?)

In 1990, I hate God.

That year, while Nocturno Culto and his band still play thrash and haven't really figured out black metal, I hate my way through every primary school classroom, and the teachers' thick southern Norwegian accent. I refuse to adopt it. I hate its sombre tone, fit only for sermons and admonitions, and southern Norwegians hardly ever utter anything else. Their accent is so formulaic and repetitive, it won't allow them to say anything new. I can't imagine it used for anything but preaching. When they say 'I'm a *pRacticing chRistian*' their guttural Rs make it sound as though the consonants have gone through purgatory. My ears are ringing with stigmata.

I especially hate *Gøud*, as people from Aust-Agder pronounce it, as my teacher recites it in early morning prayer. As I've come to understand it, *God* is a theoretical concept that only exists in books, while *Gøud*'s presence pulls southerners' hair back into tight knots and twists their throats into nooses. It's *Gøud* that records written warnings in my diary when I don't memorise the third verse of our set psalm, 'Moon and Sun'. It's *Gøud* who decides that we're not taught anything about other religions or philosophies. I hate *chuRch seRvices*, *chRistenings*, *weddings*, and *funeRals*; and I hate the way southerners pronounce them. I hate the Christian Democratic Party and the Protestant creed, I hate it off by heart, I hate it backwards and upside-down. Our Father, who art in hell.

Saying that now still makes me warm and happy inside. I'm still blasphemous. I enjoy the burning sensation of shame, when your cheeks swell and glow in the hot fire of exclusion. Even now, I identify with the little match girl from Hans Christian Andersen's fairy tale. Sitting in a freezing alley, she's warmed by images of everyone else's Merry Christmas, and just like her, I steal heat from other people's creed to warm my cold demon soul. The little match girl shivers through visions of glittering Christmas trees and angelic holograms. She tries to warm up on the ghosts of holiness, the mirage of Protestantism, and freezes to death in the attempt.

Hatred makes me so happy. My hatred is radioactive, and as a child in 1990, I beam with it.

Hatred is my imaginary world, my pleasure dome. How would you even say *pleasure dome* in Norwegian? You don't. Definitely not in a southern accent. Here my hatred exists only deep in my gloomy stare, in that look that seems about to implode, that seems to look into itself in pictures. Is that gaze the language they call hatred?

You don't have to answer, of course. You might not understand a single word of Norwegian in any accent. But maybe hatred has made you happy, too. That's why I'm writing this to you. To get away.

From the moment I learn to write, I hate God. I have to capitalise all these words, and I hate it. Jesus Christ, Our Father, God, and so on. Written submission. In school they give me extra tutoring sessions to teach me capital O. In class I just draw spirals, and they assume I can't draw a circle. During these sessions I'm supposed to sit and spell out the Word in Norwegian, *Ordet*, with a capital O, the way it's spelt in the Bible. I remember having to repeat it over and over, I remember burning inside, and I remember *Ordet* burning, and I remember finally breaking and writing a series of OOOOOOOOOOO's on the sheet, more like doodles than words. I cross all the lines on the sheet until I'm writing outside the worksheet and on the desk and the teacher returns and gives me a written warning. Have you ever thought about how similar the words *scrawl* and *scream* sound? I hate capital letters and I hate the Word.

We're not allowed to say *hate* unless it's about Hitler. Someone's

5

dad said that. But I don't say it like them anyway, *hadår*; it's too soft and wet. I say *hate*, and I love to hate. It's 1992 and I'm the Gloomiest Child Queen.

It's 1992 on the screen as well now, on the bonus material DVD that came with the reissued early Darkthrone albums. Swirling trees shot in black and white. Tense atmosphere. I follow the shaky camera around the forest, delighted by its attempt at turning the plain, pleasant and ordinary pines into something ugly, threatening and mysterious. As if the band were attempting to really squeeze the lifeblood out of 1992, or as if they're expelling the ordinary 1992 out of the year.

A boy, still Nocturno Culto I think, is smoking on a bench in the forest. 'More primitive,' Fenriz says. He's speaking English. It's an interview, done many years after the film, and the band is summarising and analysing. They're able to look back and say, We went for something more primitive.

You can watch the interview for yourself. It's online. *Primitive.* I've never heard anyone say that in a southern accent.

As I hate my way through school, to 1997 when I enter college, it becomes more and more obvious that language doesn't quite cut it. Something's wrong down here in the south. Maybe there's something wrong with the Norwegian language altogether. Maybe Norwegian doesn't have the right words or sounds to really express pleasure. It feels like a provincial language, a language only appropriate for small talk about the weather, church services, Baptist church congregations, boat manuals and sermons. It's not as musical or archaic as the words in the Old English Dictionary and ancient English poems printed in Gothic font. The Norwegian language is full of words to describe my sins and mistakes; it's my forced vernacular, a language fit for people who don't really understand language, who don't understand poetry or the need to communicate. In college I identify with Inger, a character from one of the novels on our curriculum, *Growth of the Soil* by Knut Hamsun. Inger has a harelip and a speech impediment. She can't seem to get words out properly, so instead she just shuts up, or should shut up, according to Hamsun. Her muddled speech delights me. I should probably identify with her even more. She's an expression of a genetic mutation that affects her mouth and her mind, and I probably am, too. But I don't. Instead of sympathy I choose hatred. I hate Hamsun. Especially his *Pan*, another book we're assigned. I refuse to finish it. I tell the teacher that it's an insult to the brain, and the teacher gives me a written warning. I wish I'd told the teacher that the Bible is an insult to the soul.

My whole childhood and throughout my adolescence, I'm frothing at the mouth. When I talk, and when I don't talk. When we're forced to recite Ibsen's *Terje Vigen*, the only part I identify with is the verse that describes the hard sea and frothy waves around the Homborsund reefs. That's how the inside of my mouth froths when I read. There's nothing smooth or soft in my mouth: everything that's moist froths and foams endlessly, like a looped beat.

Nocturno Culto's cigarette is out. The camera is in the forest again, black and white snow accompanied by music from *Transylvanian Hunger*. I note: 'Norwegian nature looks and sounds like buzzing, angry insects.'

I'm watching these black metal clips because I want to write a

7

film. I don't know what the film is going to be about yet, but I like the early black metal aesthetic, so near to my own childhood. Strangely, it gives me hope, hope that it's possible to make art primitively, in a way that isn't steeped in professionalism and compromise. Art that still hates. I remember how much hope there is in hatred.

The next clip I watch is a black metal gig that looks as if it took place in an assembly hall in an early nineties secondary school. I note: 'Wholesome Norwegian youths talk amongst themselves and walk in and out of the room while the band plays on, completely unaffected. Black metal crawls unnoticed through adolescence, mine too. It doesn't burrow down completely, but for as long as it's there it lives and crawls.'

One of those youths could have been me. If I'd been a few years older, or if the clip had been from 1997 and not 1991. If I hadn't been a girl and excluded from the black screen. It could have been me: we could have hated, all of us, together. Instead I had to hate alone. Provincial hatred.

The Juggler, says Fenriz in the clip. We wanted to play the Juggler.

Does he mean Jester? The court jester who turns everything upside down and transforms the world into a dark game, the comedian tasked with bringing the king the worst news? But Fenriz says *the Juggler*. It's never easy to figure out what people mean when they translate their thoughts into a different language. He also says, *bashed-out primitive shit*. Total misanthropy. *Total misanthropic black metal*.

Boys from Kolbotn, or from Sveio and Rauland and Ski, or

even Arendal: I'll show you misanthropy. I go to gigs just like the one from the assembly hall tape. I go there because I want to escape Christian Norwegian conformity and because I'm searching for a new community, outside the classroom. I'm here, too. On stage there are only boys. Boys who throw their long black hair back and forth, headbanging with choreographed precision. Not far from what I've been taught in jazz ballet. But while jazz ballet codes girlish headbanging as *sexy*, the identical movement means aggression in the metal community. Here, black is the only colour, leather and velvet are the only fabrics, and the glistening guitar necks resemble swords or dicks, or both. When I look around the gig I see only boys in the audience, or no, there are other people, too. But none of the girls are headbanging, and I'm the only one like me. No one else seems to hate. 1997 is too late. After all the murders and church arsons, metal has run scared. It has passed into a lacy romantic phase. The hatred has been prescribed sedatives. Primitive recordings of buzzing chaotic riffs have been exchanged for aggressive angst. It complements southern Norway's rainy climate, synthetic drugs and gracious reservation. No one in the room wears corpse paint. There are a couple of boys wearing black eyeliner, but they're too busy selling ecstasy to secondary school pupils to listen to the music. I'm at the back, alone, hating, motionless, muted, squeezed into a corner between action and meaning. Like you were, too, perhaps.

We never meet. Provincial hatred is so lonely. But it saves us, so we don't drown in our own frothing spit. And perhaps it saved the boys too.

I'm still working on this film. I'm writing it to figure something

9

out, or to find my way out of something. A way out of language, perhaps? In a way, that's exactly what it means to write a film. It's a document that transgresses against the written domain. The writing doesn't exist independently, but facilitates a different art form, the film; the text yields to it, as the bonus material yields to the Darkthrone albums. I think that's how I want to write: unfixedly, sloppily, impossibly—*primitive*. A script is a curse that hasn't been uttered. It's a ritual that hasn't begun. A magical document.

Maybe this document is where I should look for the primitive. Maybe this document is where I can attempt to dig something out of language, something that doesn't exist in text or image but is somewhere in between. It has to be something new, a new space. It can't just look like what has been. Writing shouldn't just be repeating instructions. Doing that has to be the very definition of blasphemy. I was never taught to hate God.

When I write, I enter and exit scenes, I see everything. I *am* God in here. I can only hate myself.

I watch again the final clip from the bonus DVD. We're in the forest again, always in the forest. The grove has darkened. Is it almost evening? Snow now. A winter forest. The guitar sounds are alien, as if they weren't recorded using a cord and a microphone. It sounds like insects that crawl and buzz all over the four-track machine.

I'm trying to write a new scene into my own film, from a party I was at once: An opinionated and skinny sixteen-year-old from Nedenes is dead set on telling everyone what Satanism really is. People are only ever really looking out for themselves, he says, so man should cultivate the idea of himself as the hero of his own life. Or maybe he's saying that Satan is just a symbol that represents our life force? He's spouting something along those lines, some stuff he's read in a book, a book that looks too much like the Bible and the Word and probably has just as many capitalised letters and just as few women's voices. No one understands what the boy is saying anyway. But a little later, when he begins to cut his belly and blood starts trickling, we understand everything. Cutting we get. We feel it in our own belly and our own skin. We identify with the cutting, and the blood from the cuts. Blood speaks a language we understand, without that broken southern accent.

A girl character of about the same age tries to help him, manages to pull the knife away and sits chatting to him. Another girl just stands there, watches it happen and later walks home from the party through fresh snow, trailing a river of blood behind her. That's supposed to represent me, obviously, the lonely bleeder. I could have walked home like that in 1997.

I scratch that scene. Too many lonely bleeders, a competition of teenage angst and loneliness. It's too psychological. I hate psychology. Psychology looks like religion, and the psychologist character looks too much like God, someone you're supposed to open up to, someone you're supposed to approach with honesty, someone you're supposed to use to break yourself to pieces, self-destruct in front of, so much so that the little splinters left behind can't even be called art. This thing called opening up is really just repeating instructions. Repeating instructions is human: lonely girl kneeling before God.

I'm sick of being lonely. I want to be part of something. I've been practicing since 1991. While Fenriz and Nocturno Culto stagger around with their camcorder and destruct the forest structures, I'm doing the same thing in my exercise books and notepads. I write my school assignments and my Norwegian essays *to* someone. Not to the teacher, but to famous authors: Ibsen, Bjørnson, Shakespeare. They frequently reply in the margins, leaving biting comments about today's youth and correcting my spelling and syntax long before I hand in the assignment, and I get a written warning: the teacher insisting in that wet southern accent that he *can't mark a paper that's already been marked.* But I continue to hate in the A4 paper margins; I do anything to avoid thinking about how I'm really writing to God, God in the guise of the teacher. I've always needed to write to someone else. Writing has to be a place, a place to meet, a place where you meet someone other than God.

The only thing I like from the party scene is the image of blood flowing: that living and dead tissue. It flows continuously, unbroken and shapeless, and it gives me hope, just like the camera that sways between pines. Blood doesn't have nationality, religion or gender. Maybe I have to rid the film of all plot and psychology and focus on blood and guts. The way black metal did at its most abstract, or when their recordings were so shoddy that the murder and Viking lyrics couldn't be distinguished from the buzzing guitar riffs or cymbals. When everything sounded like howl, a space filled with shapeless components. Maybe I have to write like that, too: blacked out.

I grew up in southern Norway's white Scandinavian paradise: white walls, white fresh snow, white painted laminate and white

chipboard, white flagpoles and white chalk lines on the black-
board, white cheese and white fish, milk, fish pudding, fish gratin
and fish balls in white sauce, white pages in books, white pills in
pill boxes, white roll-ups, platinum-blond hair, white brides and
white doctors' coats, meringue and cream cake, Christian virgins
from Jesus Revolution with white wooden crosses, Christian
grunge, listen, the music sounds like regular grunge, if you just
forget about the lyrics, irony, nothing means anything, boys from
White Revolution at summer camp, girls who think it's fine that
the boys are racists because they're hot and because boys will be
boys, boys and their Nazi punk songs, listen to this track, the
lyrics are so distorted you can't hear it anyway, listen, the melody's great, you girls are gonna love it, it's got acoustic guitar. Sugar
and salt are the only spices. Sugar and salt look exactly the same.
White revolution and Jesus Revolution, Nazi punk and evangelist
grunge, swastikas and purity rings, mid-morning gruel, pimple
pus, egg whites, cream of wheat, semen.

The word *white* even has an h in it, imagine, a hidden letter,
w*h*ite. And we let that pass, linguistically. What does it do to us,
that hidden letter, what (w*h*at) do we hide in that h, w*h*at hides in
the w*h*ite?

The white postwar period is scrubbed so clean it doesn't have
shadows, like Carl Theodor Dreyer's films. Protestant, newly rich,
superficially liberal, minimalist and modern. Southern Norway
in the late '90s is not as newly rich and a little less modern, but
just as white: It's completely acceptable to point out the rightful
supremacy of the white race. It's totally fine to call someone a
nigger, to beat up boys who look feminine in any way, or to raise

your hand and ask to leave the classroom when confronted with a lesbian teacher, because homosexuality is not respectable (*we respect you as a person and pray for your salvation*). It's acceptable to look down on those miserable wretches who aren't Christian, who aren't Norwegian, aren't white or who aren't straight. Inside that hidden *h* there are hundreds of commandments, from the ten first and onward into white eternity, ones that no one can pronounce, but everyone knows. The childhood I have left behind/tried to leave behind is like a metaphysical cesspit surrounding me, where the Christians have dumped their thoughts and their prayers for my salvation and purification.

Purification reverberates in every conversation. Dear Lord, and My Word, the evangelist Christian girls say when they're angry, because they can't say God – that would be taking the Lord's name in vain, which after all is an act comparable to murder according to the Scripture. Language shouldn't transgress boundaries, language should be tamed, you can't just go wherever, don't come here with your words. You have to keep the *h* silent.

The only thing I can do to stave off the south is to turn pitch-black and severe. I start playing in a metal band, dye my hair black, the colour of blasphemy, and dress in the darkest colours possible. I imagine that my presence in the classroom is itself destroying or disrupting something, even though the clothes I wear are what I call *provincial black*, meaning whatever you can get in dark velour or velvet, down at the friendly Arena shopping centre in Arendal. I walk the halls at school with Dostoevsky, Joyce and Baudelaire in my arms like an armoured plate across my chest. Around my neck is a chain with a black rose on it, one of the flowers of the dead, and through my headphones walking to and from school I listen to music I imagine is made in black and white. I christen the room I rent near college the witch's dorm, and hang black velvet over the curtain poles, light black wax candles and write obscene comments in tiny print in the margins of the copy of the New Testament in the drawer of the nightstand. These objects, words and symbols, all this black, are little curses, magical armour that keeps the Christianity out. I am a *provincial goth*.

The metal band also attempts to drive out the Christianity, with lyrics, guitar riffs, dark bass lines and a MIDI church organ that sounds broken, like a tonal upside-down cross. During our gigs I expect something to give, that there will come a moment when I don't have to hate so much. Instead I'm infuriated by all the mundanity I observe from the stage. The rock club's emergency exit sign, the sad seventies curtains, the cracked wood panelling painted white and green. You might as well be at a Free Church recital. The teens in the audience look ordinary, too. They talk loudly by the canteen, buy fizzy drinks, and make the till ring incessantly and cheerfully, or they headbang with open mouths in front of the stage, looking, even though they'd never admit it, like the speaking-in-tongues Jesus crowd who right this moment are praying for us at the free churches of Filadelfia or Betania and calling it *Jesus Revolution*.

The band too, is just as ordinary, just as regulated, just as hierarchical. The boys stand quietly at the back, play riff after riff on black guitars, looking down at the floor as if they were bending their necks to a higher power, and I can't go anywhere, either; if I do my microphone starts to whine and my voice disappears. I hang on to the microphone stand. I'm desperate to change it all, break out of the loop, jump into something else, something that can take me elsewhere, closer to something. I want the rock club to become a Zen temple, a medieval castle or, preferably, a Witches' Sabbath.

In 1998 I plunge 2B's college class photo into darkness. I'm in the top left corner with my black clothes and my black lipstick and at one point I'm so fed up with the photographer's encouragements to smile that I say *fucking hell*. Around me, half the class cross themselves, as if they really believe that my words will bring Satan – hell himself – down on Grimstad town centre. (Or up to? Where is he really coming from?) The very man, in flesh and blood. We're surrounded by belief in magic and transgression, by this terror that language will crush piety and Christian faith.

I hate God from 1990 to 1998, and when I say that, I adopt the same conviction, like a proper southerner: I hope that I can use language to step into the borderlands, the places in between imagination and reality, the material and metaphysical. That's why we write, to find new places, places far from the south.

The Room

Let's zoom out now.

We're in a long hallway with grey and green walls. Fluorescent lights flicker on and off in the ceiling, the paint is peeling off the walls and the floor is covered with a fine layer of dust that shimmers in the flickering light. You can hear the sound of footsteps, but only a faint echo, as if we've got lost on the abandoned set of an old social-realist film. Not just the paint, but the realism, too, peels off in large flakes.

We're in a world where only impressions are real, and the original sounds belonging to the film left the premises a long time ago. Here and now have been rubbed out, or don't exist for us.

This is where I want to write, in an impossible place, a place that no longer exists. In the void left after films made as early as 1969 (*Daisies*), and 1974 (*Penda's Fen*), and 1976 (*Jubilee*) . . . The empty studios still exist. Let's go there. Maybe there'll be other traces here, too, that no one cares about, that no one sees, that are impossible, in the margins of the film, in the perforated edges of the frames, in cut scenes, bonus material.

I want to start my own film here, in these remnants. I want to feel the moments where realism was dissolved, be part of the scenes in which unbreakable rules for narratives were

17

broken as if it were the most natural thing in the world. I want to be where they unearthed the subtle and the sublime from the primitive.

The films I'm talking about reveal the gaps in our own consciousness, the restrictive framework of our daily lives. They also show me the holes in art's paradigms of good and bad, which are just as mysterious and hierarchical as the southern evangelist norms. These films remind me of hatred, and make me value hatred, this feeling I've been told to put away by the South, God and the University, which also told me to 'open my heart,' or 'show, don't tell,' or be more subtle. They don't screen *Daisies*, *Penda's Fen* or *Jubilee* in the film classes I take at university, first in Oslo and then in New England. In the film classes, we're taught that *Citizen Kane* is the best film in the world, followed by everything that Tarkovsky and Bergman made. We're not taught about the underground. We're taught that it isn't good to be primitive and paint with too thick a brush. We're not even taught what a thick brush is. During my film studies, when I hear a teacher praise the visual motif 'plastic bag floating in the wind' in the 'masterpiece' *American Beauty* for the third time, I feel that brush, that hatred, stir in my throat and I daydream that my mouth opens and all that's thick and black comes out, not to empty me, but to paint the entire canvas black, paint over the whole plastic bag scene in *American Beauty*, paint over every movie poster and every DVD copy of the film, every Orson Welles film and why not Tarkovsky and Bergman too while we're at it, all of it, totally black, *Stalker* and *Wild Strawberries* and all that crap, get rid of the canon, bring in monochrome, a room full of formless black components. Hatred isn't subtle, but it's beautiful. Hatred is my *pleasure dome*.

Maybe Nicolas Roeg managed something that's simultaneously subtle and challenging when he made *Insignificance*. In that film, made in the mid-eighties but set in the fifties, a series of characters meet in a hotel and act out philosophical and political issues of the postwar era. The characters are fictional, but the spitting image of fifties icons: a movie star looks like Marilyn Monroe but isn't her, a professor looks like but isn't Albert Einstein, a senator resembles but isn't Joseph McCarthy, and a baseball player isn't, but looks like, Joe DiMaggio. That they are fictional copies of real people seems at first disruptive and artificial, since they look like representations of Marilyn Monroe and so on, as seen in other films. Then that impression fades, and the gap between film and reality grows increasingly complex. The characters mimic the icons but act out completely fictional scenes in which Almost-Einstein and Almost-Monroe test out each other's roles, and she retells the relativity theory with children's toys, a flashlight and balloons. When it all ends with the hotel room exploding, all resemblance to reality crumbles. This wasn't an event that really happened. It doesn't necessarily have anything to do with the plot of the film, either, aside from the time of the explosion, 08.15, the same time that the atom bomb was dropped over Hiroshima. It turns into an aesthetic feast, as toys, balloons, a flashlight and Almost-Marilyn's body are dismembered, scorched, and liquefied. The film's structure has managed to accommodate another disjointed footnote, another almost-character, Almost–*Little Boy*.

What explodes is primarily fictional. The film's plot has unfolded in a hotel room built in a film studio. A hotel room is a sort of illusory, temporary home, perhaps in the same way that the film and the film studio are a temporary home to the production of an illusory reality. When the illusion-space is blown up and the room pulverised and drizzled in front of the camera in slow motion, it's as if the film has blown the roof off the entire history of film. The illusory construction, the one that tells us we should foster real feelings for something that looks like reality but isn't, is pulled apart. Little bits of wood and metal, pillow feathers, clothing fibres, flesh, drops of blood and bits of intestines float around the room in slow motion and find new places there, like food morsels about to congeal in aspic.

Maybe the film, with this blast, also expresses a primitive desire to transform reality into fiction. Not like the blockbuster films that transform death and violence into something beautiful in the service of a Crusader politics that romanticises war, but the opposite. Here the blast is something fictional and insignificant. Perhaps Nicolas Roeg is asking, could we have blown up something fictional instead of Hiroshima and Nagasaki? If what we blew up had been fictional and the bomb also fictional, no lives would have been lost. The explosion would have had exactly the same significance to the world as the snow globe that tumbles from of the hand of the dying man in *Citizen Kane*. It would have been historically insignificant.

Could we turn back time and blast fictional Japanese cities instead of real ones? asks *Insignificance*. Could we live out our fantasies without needing to cross the line to where real people have to die? Is the problem actually our perception of reality and the cap it puts on imaginative expression? Can art's insignificant explosions blast our illusions to bits?

This is the space I want to write in, the blasted hotel room, in the long echo that follows the moment the illusion is shattered, as everything that mimics what we've been taught to call reality is ripped to shreds and drizzles down around us.

In 2005, the summer holiday after I finish my undergraduate degree in Oslo, and with it all the university's fossilised film classes, I travel to Japan. Not to Hiroshima or Nagasaki, but to Kyoto, Japan's ancient capital, known for its many temples, kimonos, teahouses and paper shops. I remember a residential area with street after street lined with small wooden houses, like a little village in the middle of the town. It's impossible to look through the windows that face the street: they are hidden behind fences, plants, or shutters, and I glide through the streets without the company of my reflection, a little more invisible and less myself than I'm used to. I understand that Japanese people like to keep things to themselves. They're secretive beings. They'd rather look down than meet my eyes, and more and more people here wear a white mask over nose and mouth, supposedly so as not to spread or receive other people's bacteria or viruses, but also to hide. They swarm around Kyoto, unidentifiable and untouchable behind their masks, like a web without connections. Their history is a long chain of disappearances, erasures and reconstructions. There are so many reasons not to exist here, or not to exist completely.

I'm given a tour of a Zen temple in the middle of town. It surprises me to see the walls, ceiling and floor looking so spotless, because the temple otherwise seems very old, and I find out I'm right, the temple is old, but the building is relatively new. It's demolished and rebuilt every fifty years. This is done to preserve the construction technique, because the craft is more important than the object it created, the temple. Maybe it's also to avoid cultivating attachment to a material thing. Or to avoid cultivating the self, and obliterating the illusion of value?

I remember this now, many years later, as though my film writing has summoned it: I remember talking to the temple guide about 'magic', never even questioning why I'm using the word at all. What do Japanese people think about 'magic', what are 'rituals', what are 'spirits'? Japan is so alien to me that it doesn't cross my mind that this is the first time I've talked about gods and spirits without feeling that hatred of the South pulse through my body. At some point the South must have let me go, or Kyoto has pushed it so far from my consciousness that I've been able to forget where I'm from. I've given up, or suppressed, the provincial black hatred.

In Japan it's so easy for me to forget to hate, to forget my entire emotional register, everything I've brought with me. Here I'm a total stranger, even to myself. I don't know a single character of the written language, and I have no idea which are used in the word *hate* or whether they even have such a word. People's behaviour here, their tradition, their religion are so different that I can't see my reflection in them. I've disappeared almost completely. If I haven't already forgotten or erased myself, I can do it here. I identify with the temple, with what's demolished and rebuilt without traces from its previous life, without revealing where it came from.

As I'm speaking to the temple guide, people keep stopping next to us, outside the passage into the most sacred room, where statues of guardian gods rest on their pedestals. As they silently pass through the rooms, cold now in February, the visitors greet the gods, or leave something for them. Later that day I realise that everywhere I've been I've also greeted something or given something or other away. I removed my shoes to enter the temple, removed the red temple slippers to enter the inner chambers, and handed my ticket to the ticket inspector. The barista in the coffee shop handed me the receipt for an espresso with both hands, and I gave coins in return, attempting to make my thank-you just as ceremonious. In Kyoto, even buying coffee has significance: I *give* something, and the weight of the action, the bow, the emphasis, gives me the feeling that I'm also giving away part of myself. I'm participating in a ritual. This is how easy and free of sin it can be, like a magical transaction, a movement to participate in.

Later that evening I practise greetings. I bow to the rooms in the apartment where I'm staying, to the hands of the waiters that pour tea in my cup at a tea house. I stop and nod in an art gallery inside a metro station, and nod to the metro station's revolving doors and to the guard smoking on the floor above me. I bow my head to the underground engine, the ticket inspectors, the drivers, the passengers that exit the metro before I get on.

It isn't until now, as I write my film many years later, that I understand that what I was doing in Japan was a form of blessing, the same action practised by the pastors of the South. In Japan, I bless the rooms, the things and the people. Maybe without knowing it I'm compensating for something I never allowed myself to do. Maybe I don't recognise the movement because it seems so easy without the Christian association. In the South, blessing seems to be about getting some sort of permission from God, a holy white stamp. I haven't had access to that type of communication. I've only learned to use the curse, its depraved twin sister, profusely. From the window in my witch's dorm, I surveyed Bible-belt suburbia, and I cursed the college, the super-market, and Kingdom Hall, the gas station, the late-night McDonald's, and car after car zooming down the motorway.

In Japan it's different. For the first time I'm able to let go of the hatred, and the first thing I do is seek out religion. I remember several other moments from the trip now. I recall a Bible shop in Tokyo that doesn't scare me; I even walk in. It looks just like a regular bookshop, except the paper quality, the binding, the forms of the books seem more sacred than their content. I remem-ber, too, how among the unfamiliar temples, gods, spirits and rituals, I feel disconnected from myself as spiritual content, as sin and soul. I can be material, elegantly formed bones, intricately packed intestines, colourful kidneys and ovaries under smooth skin cells. I exist as the parts and the whole of the beautifully wrapped food in the bento boxes. I don't need to hate all this reli-gion. I reclaim the act of blessing without thinking about it, without knowing it.

In the side panel of my film document, next to the notes on black metal, I note this: 'Writing summons the unfamiliar places.' In this place, the Kyoto I didn't know I had experienced until now, the blessing and the curse form a richer whole, an act that doesn't need to be religious. It can be magical instead: simpler, more open, taking a lower aim. I can establish a connection or a pact, demonstrated through a connect-the-dots drawing between myself and the world of the gods, the underworld, or between myself in the past tense and myself in the present. Or all of it simultaneously. Maybe I could even draw up a map between me and you.

Maybe writing this film has created a place to meet. Do you also recognise the desire for secret and impossible connections? Do you recognise the loneliness, could we share in it? Could we get closer to each other? Could you and I and the film be the start of a *we*? A *we* which takes the form of an expanding community of girls who hate?

Let's see . . . We're in a room, I think, a nondescript room. At this point it could be any room. It's still without depth, width, length or any sense of time . . . It might have other dimensions, ones we don't yet know about, dimensions that don't have names. Perhaps we're in a room with a closed centre. There, at its core, it reserves space for something else. Everything else. Maybe a room without us has room for the connections between us.

From a distance we hear voices belonging to a class of teenage girls. The murmur comes from a cold classroom at the end of the hall. We glide between the girls into the classroom, invisible, like a video camera, while they recite their names one by one. They seem to have short and simple names, but we can't hear them, only an indistinct hum. It sounds as if we're outside the room, or as if we've stopped our ears with cotton and can only hear the drone from our own heads. We have to read their lips to understand what they're saying. A girl fills the frame and introduces herself in two syllables. We can only see her lips. Maybe her name is Venke. As she says her name, icy mist escapes the corners of her mouth. Threads and bubbles of spit knot her lips together as she opens and closes them around two syllables. A weak shimmer that resembles a muted laptop gleam is coming from deep down in the girl's throat. The light escapes her mouth, filtered by her tongue and the different constellations of her teeth.

There are no windows, no bookshelves, no books, no coat racks or chalkboards around the girls. Instead, images are projected onto the spotless white concrete walls as if they were a canvas. Images of windows are projected onto the walls, with trees swaying in the wind, and images of bookshelves full of books on maths, geography, history, chemistry, Norwegian and Christianity. If it weren't for the concrete's rough surface, it might look almost real. Their school uniforms look almost real, too. They are wearing black, slightly stiff-looking jackets with shoulder pads, and matching pleated skirts, but with yellow neon stripes on their sleeves and trainers. They look like a futurist marching band.

A teacher takes attendance from behind a desk at the far end of the room. She is wearing a fitted black suit with stripes that gradually shade from red to purple to blue. She yawns a little. Each time a girl says her name, this teacher taps a screen with her right index finger. As she takes their names she also sticks each finger of her left hand into a small machine that resembles an automatic pencil sharpener. The machine sands her nails neatly and paints them a gorgeous bright pink.

We continue to watch the girls' lips move. The murmur of voices and the hum from the air conditioning make it impossible to discern individual words, but the conversation seems academic. Some lips are more energetic, they expel longer words from their mouths, working harder and producing more saliva. Other lips are softer and more questioning. Eyeshadow glitter falls on a shoulder, someone's chest, a desk; the glitter intermingles with the glare from the overhead lights.

There's a girl seated at the back of the classroom who's not quite paying attention. Everything she's wearing that isn't part of her uniform – her socks, undershirt, pants, bra – is black. She looks up from her writing. At first glance she seems to be writing in a notebook, but it's soon revealed to be a tablet. A small projector shaped like a gaping goat's head is attached to it. Light spills from the goat's mouth as if from a fountain and projects a 3D drawing of lines, text, and images onto the surface of the tablet.

The girl uses a pen to write in her book, then pushes the pen against the projection: the text disappears. She continues to think.

The girl is me, obviously. She represents my wet dream of writing myself into a story, and that includes you too, reading this. Perhaps she's me in 2002, hating God at university, spending hours attempting to make Microsoft Word occult by inverting the colours so I can write in white on a black document. I'm seething. How is this so hard? Why do we have to chisel black ink into an empty canvas? Why does white mean innocence, beginnings; why is it the colour of indexes, emptiness and poetry? Why do I have to bang my forehead against white walls and stare glassy-eyed at white forever? The only thing I want is to be able to brainstorm with colours reversed, to write with white hope on black hatred. I want to be able to begin with hate.

We return to the room. The girl in the classroom isn't a character; she's made herself invisible to the others. She's the camera in this film, a camera that also has her own feelings and thoughts.

She introduces herself with her mouth, as Terese, Terese after Theresa Russell, the actor who plays Almost-Marilyn in *Insignificance*. Terese records negative film, with colours inverted: black is white, white is black. She's not a subject, she's the eye, a thing, an object, that sees, feels, zooms, inverts. She could be you. She's a thing that hates.

Terese has always made herself invisible in this way. Pretended that she's a camera. She hasn't seen black metal videos or hung out with corpse-paint boys, but she's spent half her childhood squinting at trees and the sun, making treetops and sky swirl and darken. She spent her youth on the internet, sent information bundles of text and image back and forth over mIRC. She felt herself disappear a little more each time, as if her body no longer had a visible surface. She identified with Ally Sheedy's character in *The Breakfast Club*, the black-clad nerd who shakes her hair over her desk to make dandruff drizzle like snow. I always thought of that scene as an adolescent witch ritual, where the witch reconstructs herself and becomes an impenetrable snow globe, surrounded by thick glass walls.

The glass is a camera lens. Terese lifts one hand and curls her thumb and index finger to make an objective lens. She rests her finger-lens on her right eye and lets the camera glide around the room. The lens fixates on the girl whose name might be Venke and zooms in on her upper body.

As this takes place, I write a list in my film document's side panel. I need lists there, lists of what my intentions are with this classroom. The list opens with the phrase *science fiction*. By that I don't mean that it's set in the future or that it's dealing with dystopian technology. *Science fiction* here means an impossible place, like an alternate reality. The images look real. I imagine girls together, in a class, or in a cluster. I imagine girls hating in unison. White to black. Mystical communication, community. Ecstatic intimacy, intimate close-ups. Intimacy through the body's waste and secretions. A self-constructed network between bodies.

(like the internet before the internet)
((like the internet during the internet))
(((or underground internet)))
((((deep web))))
(((((deep tissue)))))
((((((deep web and deep tissue))))))
(((((((ecstatic deep-webian intimacy)))))))
((((((((primitive language))))))))
(((((((((I want to understand this language)))))))))
((((((((((insist that this language signifies))))))))))
(((((((((((until it signifies)))))))))))
((((((((((((for you too))))))))))))

This is the kind of room I want to show you. A world surrounded and shaped, no, reshaped, by subcultural layers. Maybe we could turn back time and create a black metal movement where only girls hate?

The girls in the classroom look up, look at each other, smile.

An episode:

Groups of girls from different classes and schools are at a railway station waiting for the next train. They chat enthusiastically, send texts and upload photos online, look at each other, smooth their hair.

The tracks start to hum, as they do when a train is approaching.

Abruptly, a girl walks to the edge of the platform. She looks down at the tracks but continues to chat to the friends behind her.

Her friends join her. Then several more groups do the same. Everyone smiles, giggles, and whispers, as they grip each other's hands and stare at the tracks. The remaining girls don't notice the row of people forming along the edge while they wait.

The train approaches the station.

The girls on the edge all count down from three and jump off the platform.

A series of thuds is heard as the train hits each body thrown in its way. The blood splatters from the track and sprays the platform, walls and ceiling and the other girls' clothes, hair and faces. It gushes so violently, it fills the mouths, eyes and noses of everyone still on the platform. The whole image is dyed red, then black.

THE END

The Band

What happens to hate? Does hate age? Can it be cured? Can you fling it off a subway platform?

In 2005, just a month after my Japan trip, I'm sitting in a university library in New England, on the other side of the Atlantic. Maybe I've been cleansed, demolished, blown up, either during the Kyoto trip or in my new existence as an exchange student, and now I feel I can delete, turn off, restart and restore myself. I've begun the master's course and I've decided that this, finally, is far enough from the Norwegian South. Now I can be a whole new person, one who isn't pitiful and primitive, one who doesn't hate. I can be a person who creates herself, a less primitive and more open being, done cursing church assembly halls and hexing the Christian students, done painting the film screen in the lecture hall black.

I'm completely consumed by this novelty that's me. I feel easy and unreal in the reading room, as though I've been digitised. I feel indistinguishable from the bookshelves I stand by, from the students I get to know or sit next to, the white laptop I've got. No one but me can observe these changes; I'm the only constant in my own life. No one but me knows that just a couple of years ago I was black-clad and dark. Now I'm so malleable, I can chew myself like gum. I can reach right into my body and change its shape, comb myself into another physical existence, as if I were made of the whipped cream on my own birthday cake. I'm white and soft now, and I am God, but who cares, I don't care about *am*, about *being*, I only care about *becoming*, about distance, about the keyboard shortcuts, about the drive away from something. I scroll down and through myself, finding less and less of the South the further and further down, or away, I get from there. It's not here. In the new me, I can put it away, finally.

I'm someone else now, a stranger. Lots of people think I'm Swedish or Danish. I don't correct them. I only stretch as far away as possible from the Southern hatred, as far away from the original version of myself as I can take myself. I work on white paper that I no longer try to paint. I worship canonised films now, films that I previously would have been sceptical of, and I read novels that I wouldn't have touched in college. I don't protest, only smile, while the professor tells me, since I'm Norwegian, that Hamsun, pronounced *Ham Sun*, ham and sun, is one of the greatest writers in history. I'm far enough from where I came from not to care, and mature enough. I accept and respect the professor's perspective; maybe Hamsun could be *Ham Sun* to me too. I'm efficient, productive and positive; it's as if I shook my head and my hair shed its black pigment.

In the years that follow, after I'm done with the degree and with New England and I'm back in Oslo, this process continues, flowing from my graduate education into the art I create. My expression slides into the traditional, with a soft appearance and a blurred and beige presence, as if from unknown origins. I work

34

alone – freelance, independently – on my own expression. The only thing I don't like seeing written about me is that I'm from the South. It feels like a factual error, after five, then ten and, even later, fifteen years of emigration. Calling me a Southern Norwegian reintroduces this set of shadows, a collective and dirty presence that I've rinsed from myself. Did I not scrub it from my CV? Is it still there? A few years after earning my masters I go back to the U.S., and at one point in New York, I get a new laptop with an American keyboard, to get rid of æ, ø, and å. When I turn it on for the first time, at a café in Chinatown, I can feel my body tingling, as if I've woken up from a plastic surgery that has removed my old features (æ, ø, å) and made my face unrecognisable and impenetrable. Or is it the opposite? Is it the black pigments I feel tingling, and the hatred that has returned?

At first the absence of those keys on the machine feels reassuring, but then it starts to bother me. Have I used my inadequate keyboard to create my own version of the silent *h* (silent æ, ø, å)? I add keyboard shortcuts to find the letters again. By pressing several buttons at once I can bring up nonexistent signs, as if I've concocted a witch's brew that summons spirits from the underworld. A lonely Å remains, flickering on my screen in a new document that's never saved, a red line wriggling underneath it, since the writing program doesn't have a Norwegian spell check. Å, wrong.

Let's see . . . I'm sitting here with the pitiful Å, the last letter of the alphabet that no one in the café can read, the invisible letter outside the reach of the keyboard, the letter that fell off the edge of civilisation, the muffled sound, the genetic speech

35

impediment. The keyboard combination, the ingredients of it, summon more than just the letter; they evoke the black from the subconscious, the underground and the underworld. We sit here, the Å and I, at the café in Chinatown, as time speeds up around us, new customers come and go and chug from big American coffee cups filled with the countless choices of coffee that American cafés have to offer. It gets dark and light and dark and light; the café closes and opens and closes and opens. Only the laptop screen is lit with its progressively bigger, blinking Å, coming closer and closer, as if it were falling from the sky and ushering in the apocalypse. The three heralds of the apocalypse: Æ, Ø, Å.

When I get up from my chair and leave the café, I'm in the present, and the premises have moved. The computer is no longer new, and the café is no longer in Chinatown, but in Grønland in Oslo, where the customers drink from small espresso cups and glasses. The laptop screen has gone black, the Å and I have fused completely. I, who spent years creating myself and my artistic identity, I, who attempted to rub out where I came from by emigrating from my own history, have brewed myself together again from the ruins of the keyboard shortcuts.

Now I'm tired, tired of representing myself. I'm so tired of starting every sentence with 'I . . .' Actually, I'm tired of representing anything at all, alone, and of feeling that I'm competing on my own against everyone else. It's as if all the travelling and all the art meant nothing. Despite everything I've brought with me from the South this idea that I'm a sinner, and even though I don't think about God or Christians anymore, I've gone further in that idea than any of them. Sin is still inside me; everything is my fault and my responsibility, because I'm doomed to be alone, locked inside this subjectivity. I am so tired of chasing after it, this subjectivity, looking for something that's all mine, that doesn't have any context, surroundings or background. It's so lonely. It's so limited. It's so heavy. The subject is reflected negatively, the subject is so alone, so threatened, so scared, so dying, so guilty. I walk toward the Munch museum, toward the exhibition opening I've been invited to, while I think about how I want to swap some of these negatives in myself for something else, something shared. I want to take part in a chaos of collective energy. I want to be in a band.

The word BAND is quite similar to the word BOND. Have you thought about that? A band is a bond between people. A band can emerge unexpectedly, when you talk or suddenly say the same things, or mention the same references. You harmonise in conversation, create rhythm. That's the beginning. We can dive into that beat; the beat is more alive than we are. Our hearts might stop beating in the end, but the pulse of that heartbeat will continue to symbolise time, breath, life, even after we're gone. It's that simple. All we can do to feel alive is to dive into the beat, take part in it. Some might call it dancing, but the beat doesn't necessarily build up to something regular; it's changeable, and we let go and follow it, it's there, a shadow cast both by ourselves and by eternity, continuing to spread.

In this *bond* (in Norwegian the word includes the impossible letter Å, which I can now only write with an illogical character combination on my American keyboard), I can be part of something, I can be less myself and feel less trapped and dying and tucked away in my own body. My body can expand, search for others, be a part of them, become something else together, something that can live on after all the I's are dead. When I die, I want to be part of a bond, get rolled into the bond, as though dying were stage-diving off the ledge and sensing someone there to catch you.

The magic of community, of the defeat of death and loneliness. Å, I've missed you.

Venke, Terese and I are a band from the moment we meet at the exhibition opening at the Munch museum and get talking. The tone of the conversation changes abruptly from polite and introductory to witty and dynamic. We realise we can talk about the same stuff, totally relaxed and therefore at terrifying speed, without breaks; we've jumped into a jet stream that's so powerful, we don't notice that the event is over until the museum is empty and we are pushed through the doors out into the darkness.

In the days that follow the opening we continue the conversation on all the applications of the internet. We leave a chain of invisible but glittering email threads, Instagram group messages, and iMessage bubbles behind us. Even when we don't get back to each other for a while, I can feel the stream, the energy; imagine the speech bubbles being produced. Venke calls it the phantom conversation. I call it *songs*.

I call it songs because we can speak openly and without fear. Our conversations always flow continuously, safe and at the same time elastic, steady like the beat of a bass drum and fleeting like cymbals and gentle percussion. Most of all, there's a harmony, a flow of compassion that opens our currents to each other, bringing us closer together. We write and talk ourselves into each other. We become songs, together.

The first thing we talk about, right away when we meet at the exhibition, is Munch. After a while the conversation touches on one of his paintings not featured in the show, *Puberty* (1894–1895). In this painting, a very young girl sits naked on a bed, with her arms loosely crossed over her crotch. Her body casts a big, dark shadow that hits the wall behind her. The shadow looks unnatural, as if it's not coming from her but from something separate from her, something hanging over her.

It's summer and peak season when I visit the National Gallery and look at this painting. There's such a crush of people between me and the girl as I move toward her that I can only see her head, and she looks as if she were dressed. When I finally reach her, it hurts to see her naked body surrounded by the tourists' incessant clicking and yapping – tourists with their waterproof trainers, windbreakers and sensible backpacks crowding her bed, her shadow and her skin. It turns the painting into pornography, an illustration of the commercial exploitation and determined conservation of paintings with naked young women as motifs, or what we call 'art'.

But maybe the girl from *Puberty*, and all naked young women in all paintings, are actually sitting there hating. Hating the painter, hating their boring gloomy life, hating the king and the president and the bishop and the prime minister and the authors and society and their own place in it. Maybe it's not a shadow climbing the wall behind her, but smoke from the spontaneously ignited occult fire of hatred.

I'm struck by the naïve notion of taking the girl home, painting clothes on her, black clothes maybe, painting her into a new framework, as the Canadian writer Aritha van Herk does to Anna Karenina in *Places far from Ellesmere*. In this book, van Herk wants to save Anna from being another woman character in literary history who's crushed by a train, and she plucks Anna from Tolstoy's novel and gives her a new frame, a new text. She demonstrates how literature and art can tamper with their own past, create new bonds. As far as I know, no one has tried this witchcraft on Munch and his *Puberty* (she doesn't even have a name), but now I want to paint or rewrite the girl in the painting, save her, save us. Because it's definitely just as much about me, about saving myself from the position of a contemporary subject passively accepting the narratives offered it by past art, past stories about gender, expression, hierarchy. I want to save myself from nodding in acknowledgement to Munch, to 1890, from the outside, with insight, and accepting that *Puberty* is the mirror art has installed for me.

Aritha van Herk refused to accept the idea that artworks are static and complete and that stories can't be edited. She brought Anna with her, out of *Anna Karenina*, when she left her home in Alberta for Ellesmere, an island up north in Canada. Up there, far away from Tolstoy's hands, in the white icescape, the geographically blank map, she could write a new story. Facing *Puberty* and her flickering shadow, I think about my studies in New England, about how I, too, wanted to re-create myself, to save myself from the South. But I was alone, without an Anna or *Puberty*; I had no art, no more ingredients. I couldn't form any bonds, had no ability to resist new authorities or the traditions in the American university system. Here at the National Gallery in Oslo, with Venke and Terese and our electric conversation at the back of my mind, it isn't just about getting away from our homes. It's about finding bonds strong enough to tamper with both art history and our own history. It's about no longer being the match girl, the one standing outside looking in at society, with insight, in the light from the little flickering flame. I'd rather use that match to ignite the occult fire of hatred.

I've been taught to think far too much about the autobiographical, about what could be called private or even weak in the art that rewrites other art. As if how close the 'I' is to reality overshadows all other questions. Shouldn't we rather think about the bonds that are formed, that connect us? I imagine the shadow of *Puberty*, the bond, stretching out toward me and embracing me, enveloping me in its flame. In this connection, art is a magical place where reality and fiction finally are just the end points, not the underlying substance, they are full stop and capital letter, comma and line break, while the place that actually emerges, that's what's magical.

This is what fascinates me: not writing as art, I've spent my whole adult life trying to understand that, never figuring out what it is, for that I'm too primitive or inadequate to understand. But writing as magic, that appeals to me, and writing as the creation of bonds and bands, that I can understand. Connect-the-dots drawings and the invisible links between them. The band is a desire to blaspheme the beloved icons of the art institutions; a desire to save and be saved, and to rewrite: the desire not to be a passive recipient.

I haven't considered my work blasphemous since my early student days. Many years have passed since I told myself I hated God. I've never thought about magic. But in the days following my visit to the National Gallery, all this is woven together in my head, and on my old American keyboard I create a new document and begin to write something, a film, without a commission or a project in mind. The first thing I do is type Æ, Ø and Å, again and again, internalising the keyboard shortcuts as if I were playing a theme on the piano, again and again. Suddenly I'm sitting studying the old black metal clips on the bonus DVD in the Darkthrone records. Now I feel all that black returning, as if it never really left me, as if everything I've done to reinvent myself as mature and subtle and a natural creamy blond has been completely eradicated with a tiny click. The black metal clips make me want to start a new band, not to play music but to start creating something here, in community, in bonds, in hatred, in the simplified complexity of swirling tree tops in black and white, in the pixelated fractals. The creation has to begin with blasphemy, the hope in hatred. I have to get back there.

In blasphemy there's a secret pact, a desire for a community that isn't rooted in the Christian, Southern spirit. Blasphemy protects us against the moral fables we grew up with; blasphemy renounces anything that requires our submission. It shows us a crack in this reality, through which we can pass into another, more open meeting place. Blasphemy has not forgotten where it came from; it maintains that defiance and energy. Blasphemy looks for new ways of saying *we*. And the band is a we, a community that happens without anyone asking. It's an unknown communal place, an impossible place. In a place like that, we can make art magic.

A few days after we first meet at the museum, Terese and I receive an email from Venke inviting us over for coffee and a duel. Terese replies enthusiastically, saying that she's bringing her metaphorical sword, and asking for milk, sugar and biscuits with the coffee. I send a link to a book in an online bookshop as my reply. It's the book on the band Hellhammer: *Only Death Is Real.* The black metal bonus material relates to everything, it sticks to everything in me, and in us.

In the book, Tom Gabriel Fisher recounts how Hellhammer's members, later regarded as the most important forerunners to Scandinavian black metal, used to stage sword fights in the middle of the night at a traffic crossing in the Swiss suburbs. At that time they spent their evenings rehearsing and recording cassettes, while working menial day jobs in garages and factories. The band members, sick of the stifling Central European post-war era, had to invent their own rituals, and the music, inspired by heavy metal, punk and lots and lots of hatred, was the catalyst.

They put on costumes and hid by the traffic lights late at night, and when a car stopped for a red light they charged into the street and started to fence, stopping only when the car got a green light.

This was the early eighties, long before there were live-action role players or metallers in black capes and medieval outfits, and seen up close through a thin car windowpane, it must have been a frightening and absurd sight.

Driven by anger and the urge to rebel, Hellhammer's members wanted to play the part of knights on that boring suburban stage. They wanted to find meaning in an existence marked by submission, quietude, conformity and tradition. The sword fight was band practice, a gig, a protest against uniform everyday life and the hopelessness awaiting them in modern adulthood. Their battle was fought on the streets, in front of warehouses, shops, housing estates, parking lots, garbage dumps and the Swiss Alps.

After reading the book I had a clearer idea of that role-playing scene than of Hellhammer's music. At first I thought it was because sound is more difficult to describe, or that I didn't understand the music well enough, but there's another reason. Sword fights feel like complete rituals, almost like activism. They are problematic and violent, but also absurd and distinctive. Music, on the other hand, is accommodated in existing formats like records and gigs, and the descriptions of how Hellhammer found its musical expression are saturated with references to other bands and genres. As musicians, its members are defined by their instruments, their references to other bands, and the hope that their band will lift them up a level in the hierarchy and empower them.

I think about my metal band in 1998 and the disappointment I felt at the banality of the concert format and the concert venue. I think about hundreds of solo shows and projects in the years to come, and the constant pressure of conformity on what I hoped would be another word; the predictability of set lists, the pattern of the album format, the stage edge and stage times and tickets and merch and budget and ads. Hellhammer's music was created under that pressure, and Norwegian black metal, too, but bands were also formed outside music – bands formed by bonds. The bands' actions turned violent and tragic, but it could have been different. The other bands, beyond music, could have been art.

I note in my film document, 'A band is a desire for blasphemy against the disciplines.' I desire a ritual, multidisciplinary, intricate form of expression where technique and genre and subjectivity and other predetermined systems are subordinate to the community, or the desire to hate together.

Oslo seems different now. It's as if I can look down at the ground and see straight into the soil. History is there, in ever-changing strata, layer after layer of subculture from different eras.

It's been twenty-five years, thirty years, since the golden age of black metal, and even longer since Hellhammer's activist knighthood. Even for me, almost twenty years have passed since I dressed in a cape and searched in vain for black lipstick at H&M. The world is different now. Our corpse paint has long since streaked our cheeks, run into the Alna river and through Lodalen valley, under the train tracks and Schweigaards Street and into the neoliberal brackish water in Bjørvika.

Our hair, which for most of us at some point was long and black, mine even on my driver's licence photo, and was modelled on capes or lowered stage curtains, has returned to the colour of its roots; our hairlines have receded; strands from our bald spots have run down the shower drain, down to the underground where they came from. My hair was cut short a long time ago and its black chemical pigment is history. Our provincially black clothes were long ago donated to charity shops, Christian thrift shops with a saviour complex.

We're in Oslo now, and our past is mostly invisible. Our black sign language is broken, hidden away or drained into the sewers

47

along with cocaine traces from Western Oslo, traces of performance drugs from Sognsvann Park and heroin from Grønland. Even the Old Town tilts and slides down toward the Barcode development in the fjord. Subculture always flows downhill, backward. Black metal is world famous now, but it has washed itself clean of subculture, the way social democracy rinsed off socialism. Black metal isn't black anymore, it isn't a protest or a warning, it comes dressed in brawnier, more mythical and commercial colours.

But soon our band is complete, our band which is neither brawny nor mythical, but runs over, flows down in spirals to the underground. Around us Oslo East crumbles, corrodes, rots and sinks. The band makes bricks, concrete and steel beams, the places where the city is joined together flake. We pull the structures down with us.

Venke has been standing next to me, staring at the school building where we agreed to meet. Now she follows me along the school's fenced perimeter, a duffle bag dangling from her back. We've been trying to remember what questions we were set in the Norwegian exams at college. Venke claims to remember something about climate change and science fiction, but college exams were long ago, and we remember them incompletely, sometimes so incompletely that I wonder if we're confusing the essays we wrote with our real experiences.

I'm pretty sure I remember writing about Norwegian fairy tales. The text I chose was the fairy tale that frightened me the most during my childhood, 'The mill that grinds at the bottom of the sea.' Venke doesn't even remember it. She's sitting on a bench in the sun now, with her arms on the backrest and legs stretched out in front of her. Terese hasn't arrived yet. The fairy tale, I say, is the story of two brothers who take turns owning a mill that one of them acquired in a trade with the devil himself, in hell. The mill can grind anything the owner wants, be it Christmas dinner or gold, and in the end it gets stuck and can't be stopped, and one of the brothers almost drowns both himself and his entire family farm in herrings and gruel. It was this drowning motif that scared me the most, more than hell and the devil: the scene where you suffocate in traditional, grey pale Norwegian home cooking.

Maybe this is what I've had to travel to get away from my whole life. Herrings, gruel and God.

There's Terese. Three sisters.

Where are we going? asks Terese.

Hell, says Venke, and I laugh as I always do at the word hell. It's got to be the South that returns and still exists in me, the hope in hatred.

We're on our way now. Our feet step on the hard asphalt, but also on something soft. Had this been winter it could have been snow, but the snow has melted, and we're the only ones who can feel it. We're in the centre of a sea of invisible herrings and gruel. It's the refuse from all the white, fermented, rotten and aging stuff. We've spent hundreds of years perfecting a totally airtight method for flushing out and down our own dregs and decay. Even the mill winds up in the sea when the fairy tale ends.

But everything leaves traces, memories or ghosts. The mill still grinds at the bottom of the sea. It grinds out an endless supply of herrings and gruel, or black oil for what they call the Norwegian Oil Adventure. It grinds, scratches, simmers and crawls. The Scandinavian minimalist greed surfaces under our shoes.

Trash, the modern cousin of the overflowing gruel, drifts through the streets of Oslo. On the supermarket shelves it begins as an exemplar of our contemporary Pietism: sober portion packaging, proclaiming extra vitamins, low fat and sugar, pasteurisation and homogenisation. The packaging containers are safe, clean and hygienic. Eco-labelled with God's blessing. Now, if you just look closely, they're transformed into a congestion of sour cardboard, slimy plastic and sharp rusty metal scraps that rot openly in the cityscape. What once gave form to our grey-white groceries, to skim milk, oats, brown bread and fish pudding, is now semi-translucent, porous, and compressed. All the text and all the colour has been washed from its pale plastic skeleton. Most people don't see it as clearly as we do; they only notice ordinary litter and a whiff of sour wind. For us, the image of Grønland's streets appears in double exposure: contemporary world and ancient symbols. It's as if we're caught in the aura, that phase before the migraine when you hallucinate or see multiple worlds on top of each other, or before a serial killer commits another murder. This has to be the Norwegian aura: two worlds on top of each other, the real and the waste of the real.

A new double image is exposed: the Pietistic and the Occult, the glowing snow in the woods and the whirling, dark tree crowns, the purified subjectivity and the piercing hatred. Here lies that old Southern aura, layer on layer, the Christian and the blasphemous, the white and the black. The black threatens to crack open the white: the unceasing threat of heresy. The black spots are white's problem. This is what we're stretched between. What they call light, and what they call darkness, the ground and the underground, hell, amen!

We want to move the underground up a notch. Hell is a place on earth.

We walk down Tøyen. Under our feet is Oslo, southern Norway, the South, in ruins, layer upon layer of refuse and faeces, fossils of Norwegian folk tales, paintings and monopolies on food production. And below that are the archives of the underground, mile after mile of blood.

From the chain coffee shop, or from Venke's apartment, you can spy on the American metal tourists getting off the 37 bus at the Oslo Street stop to visit old Helvete, the record shop, now called Neseblod, nosebleed. A lot of them come here after reading that crap book *Lords of Chaos*. Unsure about what exactly it is they're looking for, they stand there in their cute leather jackets and collars, peering across the road before they cross it and enter the shop to buy jumpers with printed band and record logos.

Sometimes I spot black-haired couples with pierced lips and DEATH written in fake gothic font on their denim jackets, buzzing around in the streets below the Munch museum. Smart phones in their hands and map apps on the screens, they search confusedly for the apartment where Varg Vikernes killed Øystein Aarseth in 1993. Once in a while they get as far as ringing the doorbell. When *Lords of Chaos* was made into a film the producers wanted to shoot it there, to make it more authentic. But they would have found an entirely ordinary Oslo apartment with a cosy living room and kittens playing around chair legs and burrowing into the sofa cushions (they are lords of chaos, too), and a window with a view right into the botanical garden, Oslo's 200-year-old root system. If you stand by Venke's window and look to the right, you can just make out the herb garden through the beech leaves where liquorice root, lavender, vervain and agrimony are intertwined in a witch's brew. Drink this brew daily, to ward off unnecessary masculine problems.

The sun has been shining directly on the flat for hours, and inside the air is dense, like the air in a tomb furnished with our belongings. Venke opens the window, pulls out the coffee machine and pours water into the kettle. Terese slumps on the couch in the living room and opens her laptop. I'm in the hallway reading a message on my phone, then I put the phone in sleep mode and kick off my shoes. If a line were drawn between us, we'd form a triangle pointing into the flat:

hallway
me
kitchen   living room
Venke   Terese

Or, explained in band terminology:

me
guitar
Venke   Terese
bass   drums

The triangle is a simple shape, but more complex than the simplified binary that language is stuck in. The triangle is always expanding. It always opens up to a multiplicity that branches out in our subconscious. When we introduce that third component, we no longer have only a mirror image, but depth, or a magical symbol, creating portals to other places. What happens to two counterparts if you add a third? It becomes hard to define what the third component is; it could represent a sea of different possibilities. Reality, fiction, *and?* Man, woman, *and?* The presence of this third point makes the counterparts tremble.

We flip the triangle and point the tip down. This is the first shape we find on the body, and the most magical: the dark triangle of pubic hair. We step into the magical, with the trash, the underground and the shadows.

The root of all witchcraft is in this first magical shape. The magic lies deep inside, far away from the South, far away from Oslo and Norway, and at the same time so near that you can stretch out your hand and pluck some wilted grass for your witch's cauldron from the exit to Grimstad on the E18 highway. Magic is far away, because it's a place where God can't see you, I think; that's how we can find each other there. We leap out of the sinful, lonely subjective and into something that's somewhere else. In that place I'm no longer subjective, but subversive. In that place I can write. I can write because language is allowed to transcend and transform. It's the film's place, and it's the band's place.

Strictly speaking, *band* is probably not the most accurate classification language has for us, but *witches*. In the old days some called us *beldams – belles dames*. That probably carried a more positive charge and could've made a cutesier band name, but we honestly think that's too much about appearances and not enough about magic. *Witch* is the more commonly used term anyway.

Definition: 'Witch represents that which defies God.' Definition: 'Witch represents the ideological being that symbolises everything capitalism has had to destroy.' All in all, we're pretty pleased. Witches were the first band, but no one calls us a band, because a band is a transgressive community. A community like that can't take the blame for anything, and blame is what we're supposed to take.

Traditionally the world has been seen as a series of binaries: inside and outside, living and dead, man and woman, fact and fiction, science and witchcraft . . . (We know all this, Venke, Terese and I, and you probably know it, too; it's obvious, it's 'reality'.) Power, too, needs an antithesis, an 'it' or a 'her' that can be a container for everything that has threatened it. The witch is that container; she's the one who threatened the church, God, Christianity's domination, the establishment, emperors, kings, barons, Freemasons, medical science, philosophy, logic, brute strength. The deciding characteristic of a witch is: she hates God.

I move on from looking at '90s Darkthrone to poring over old books on witchcraft, studying the language used to describe the witch, her transformation, her art and her crimes. A lot of effort has been put into these definitions. Since the witch is the symbolic antithesis of power, her existence has to be constantly accounted for, and the threat she poses justified. The witch hunts of the seventeenth, eighteenth and nineteenth centuries mostly targeted women, and as a result a lot has been written about why women more often *become* witches. The witch is most often referred to as *she* and *her*. The old scriptures claim that witchcraft has to be more accessible to women. Some describe the witch as dormant in all women, intrinsic to woman's nature. Others, later, claim that only certain kinds of women perform those devilish rituals. The real rituals are where the transformation happens, where witches swear that they really do hate God, with both soul and body, and in the presence of Lucifer and other witches. *Witch-begat.*

I read that the laws concerning witches and witchcraft were usually interpreted by secular courts of law, not the Church. Maybe that's why it seems as if most of the people burnt at the stake during the witch trials were those who had challenged the establishment in some way. Political rebels, disobedient wives, shamans, midwives, unmarried lovers, agitators, Sámi people, and other people who threatened the position and prerogatives of church or kingdom, were singled out, persecuted, prosecuted and convicted as sorcerers.

What's supposed to perish when these women are convicted and burnt at the stake? What is it that must go up in smoke? It usually boils down to two words: *communal resistance.* The fire is symbolic as well as real, meant to inspire social as well as bodily fear, to weaken any lingering resistance in the remaining population. The witch trials are in many cases associated with the establishment's own fears of revolts by the common people and the strengthening of collective movements. They take place at the time of the emergence of capitalism, a period when ideologies had to be shared and developed without provoking any particular resistance in order to be established. The new theories of society include not only religion and the nation state, but also value production, exploitation of workers, and definitions of paid and unpaid labour.

Women's work becomes a crucial problem within capitalism because reproduction is seen as nonwork. Reproduction as mystery isn't new, but in capitalist rhetoric the mystery surrounding reproduction is redefined in economic terms, so that childbearing becomes not necessary but personal, a private rather than public concern, something that 'belongs behind closed doors', not labour performed but a 'natural resource' (making women generally 'natural resources,' too). These ideas and distinctions are pretty much the pillars of capitalism, of a capitalism that aims to become itself a mysterious, natural and uncontrollable force (that is, God). This is how definitions are created that decide what constitutes paying work, and what isn't actually work and therefore cannot be paid: all based on ancient cultural and religious prejudices that profit the powerful. In one stroke, a hierarchy is also created that determines which *people* can be paid or should be paid the most. At the same time, linguistic hierarchies develop between clearly defined tasks and tasks that are less quantifiable, more social, less valuable, in all kinds of labour. Work produced in bonds isn't work. Not even in art. The band isn't work, either.

Reproduction, this work that isn't work and that can't be paid, is oddly tangled up in theories about witches. During the witch trials it was constantly pointed out that witches aren't fertile and that childlessness itself could be proof of witchcraft. Fertility (the ability to *be* impregnated and *re*produce, not the ability to produce, or create), itself the proof of womanhood, is what the witch sacrifices in the pact she enters into with the devil.

Instead of bearing children, witches are said to devour them, or sacrifice them to the devil, and to enchant men into impotence. They are tried for the following: murder, abduction, causing impotence, cursing, hexing and not giving birth, all paraphrases of the greatest sin: resisting power, asking questions, hating God.

But what if these divisions ceased to exist? What if you stopped drawing a distinction between women and witches, between production and reproduction? What if you no longer separated arts and crafts from witchcraft? What if you examined what happens in the bindings, in the channels, in the blasphemy, in the dark triangles?

That's our band.

The whole world could be our witch's dorm.

We stay only partially visible now. We keep to the underground, in the shadows, in the apartment, as we plan the future, our future as a band.

The triangle rests.

Venke can be seen sleeping by the kitchen table with a tablet on her belly. Terese is hunched over her laptop, and I open the coat closet and stare into the darkness, thinking about the girl from *Puberty* and her shadow.

I give her a place on the page here, and hope I don't insult her. I just want to be close to something by being close to someone, and if I'm near her, I can perhaps be a little less primitive and pitiful; I can open up and get even closer to Venke and Terese, other people, you. Perhaps *Puberty* could rub a little paint off on me. Her pigments – the red and white flecks in her skin, the black background, the brown bed frame, are made from rock and metal oxides. They look like the colour charts of my own skin, my skeleton, my organs.

Or maybe it's her shadow bringing us together, that smouldering texture up against the wall that's so easily folded up nicely and forgotten inside a psychological metaphor or an expressionist historical detail. We step into it, into this space that's dark and a little thicker than air. The hatred gathers into a compressed texture. There's so much hope in here, hope that the shadow will finally get so dense that you could take it with you, or hope that you could mount it, step up off the ground and get out of here and into somewhere else. Maybe, inside this shadow, I could get closer to you, maybe in there we could change our own texture, get something and leave something behind, in a place between imagination and reality, life and death, myself and the world. We could hate together.

The palms of my hands are sweaty now, and my breath a little too quick; the way it gets when I stick my hands a little too far down into fiction, or too far off in the margins. I look increasingly like a cartoon character, sketched in a few lines, or perhaps more like that accelerating, sleepless online network. The internet is everywhere and reminds me of midmorning gruel filling up the house. Gruel is fairy tale blood, or fairy tale Wi-Fi.

Rats rummage in the basement under Venke's apartment. They always find another impossible way into the basement storage. Even though rats don't know about capitalism or the internet or contemporary Oslo, they know the only thing necessary, the thing I also seek. They know the underground, the ways in, the colours and the walls, and they understand how the world expands in the spit bubbles, in the uneven surface between canvas and dried oil paint, in the air pockets between our hands when we hold them, in the spaces between us; there's always space.

We follow the rats. The rats are always just ahead of us. First come the rats, then comes the plague, call-response, and it's never just one rat. The rats are a band; rats are always plural. Rats are always *we*. Ghosts, gruel, aura, fantasy, magic.

An episode:

A band composed of six girls plays in a bowling alley with gloomy lighting. They are dressed in black and the music they play gradually becomes darker and slower.

Suddenly their instruments are made of paper.

The girls begin to touch their instruments as if they don't understand what just happened.

They pick up pairs of scissors from the floor and begin cutting up the instruments instead of playing them. The music continues as if nothing has happened.

Suddenly the girls are made of paper, too.

The girls look at their scissors, smile, turn toward each other in pairs and cut each other's throats in one synchronised snip. Their heads topple off their bodies and massive amounts of red fibre silk paper streams from their empty necks.

THE END

The Gig

Where is God?

God is in the knitted hats of the humble billionaires, the heirs' sailboats, and the shareholders' velvet-lined inside pockets. God is in the pillboxes and the protein powder at the gym. God watches over the reality TV producers and the media corporations' financial advisers. God surfaces in the threshing machines separating bad art from good art. God's hand rests protectively over the hand that slaps your arse at school, at the rock club, at the university and on the underground. Because God is always in the system, in the sewers, in the trash, in the garbage. With the whores and the poor, like they teach us in school. In the 1990s the word *whore* is used frequently in the South; it's apparently biblical enough to be used in public. Society's trash. God looks after them, though. That's why it's good to be poor and exploited. You're closer to God that way; you know better than others what it's like to live. You're a straight-talker. And God's a straight-talker, too, Let there be light, he says, and there was light, and now the sun rises over the hills and the rooftops and the car parks and tints the hoods of cars and the pedestrian's intestines.

It's early morning, sometime during the spring of 2016. We've just finished our first project inside the rock under Ekeberg Hill.

This is our band's first gig. With copper bit, death knells, mistletoe and scans of the root system in the botanical garden, we've cooked up a razor-thin infected metal thread that we've pushed into one of the city's main reserves. It doesn't interrupt the internet or the electricity, and it emits no more sound than a faint peep. Only particularly attentive dogs can hear our gig, and right now they are still waiting patiently for their owners to wake up and take them out for a morning walk. But you're not supposed to hear anything, either. We summoned smell with our incantations, not sound. We've asked for the silent *h* to manifest.

Our result oozes from the mountainside and continues to do so for the next two years. Colloquially it becomes known as *the trash stench*, because it smells like rotten milk and wet dog. But the smell isn't trash or animals. It's metaphysical waste. Just as a percentage of the dust in our homes is our own hair and skin, the smell comes from internet waste, from email after email of generic asylum application rejections, cuts in social services, social housing rent hikes, press release after press release from government spin doctors. We've made porridge out of metaphysical pimple pus. Right now, even God is wading in it out there. Call it our little noise project, our little wool factory.

Frequent updates about the trash stench pop up on news apps throughout the following year:

UNEXPLAINED SMELL IN OSLO

and later

IS THE SMELL HERE TO STAY?

SMELL EXPERTS CRACK THE STENCH CODE

TIRED OF STINKING

THE TOURIST INDUSTRY IN TROUBLE

ESTATE AGENTS FEAR HOUSING MARKET STENCH-COLLAPSE

CITY COUNCIL HIRES TECH GIANT FOR STENCH INVESTIGATION

and

FINANCIAL SECTOR SPONSORS STENCH INVESTIGATION WITH MILLIONS

The final update, a year later, is

TECH GIANT ON THE TRASH STENCH: BENIGN BUT SERIOUS ENVIRONMENTAL TERRORISM FROM UNKNOWN CRIMINAL NETWORK

In the article the private investigators emphasise that while the stench hasn't brought with it any measurable air pollution, they fear that it creates worry and confusion in the population, and so they are developing new tech to improve air quality as they investigate this unknown criminal network. They add, 'We believe that we can reverse negative tendencies in social development using the right technology. The right technology could, we maintain, be the answer to questions usually regarded as social issues.'

That last sentence automatically produces an extra puff of stench above central East Oslo. An invisible cloud brews down in Grønlia, only to travel against the wind towards Bjørvika, making good time, and seeping into every air vent in the new Barcode development. It's a start: a slow, modern church arson, but we need more. We need sound.

Black metal. What is it, when did it begin?

1993, says Terese. Church arson and killings.

1987, says Venke. Mayhem releases their first EP, *Death Crush*.

1981, I say. Hellhammer's knight rituals and cassette tapes.

Trash the year then, and let's stick to Norway, says Venke. True Norwegian black metal.

Is it perhaps the closest we ever got to rebellion? someone asks.

Rebellion against what, someone responds, Norwegian Christian culture? It was just a couple of teenage boys.

Young Munchs, says the third, and all three feel the presence of the *Puberty* girl. She's a Munch after all, painted half living, half dead. Munch's people are exactly that, *corpse paint before corpse paint*, no real human underneath, nothing either living or dead.

Black metallers didn't invent corpse paint; it has existed since the dawn of pigments. They didn't even invent the Norwegian expressionist version. But they reinvented the technique as a postmodern teenage ritual, like a social medium before social media. They invented it for themselves and put their own living human faces underneath. Through this transformation we didn't become just living dead, but also icons, tools for communication, apps.

The mask was more real than my own face, a body part that was only partly my own, and only partly carried my sins. I was death, my own and others'; I was unrecognisable behind the white and black, as we all become unrecognisable when all our muscles relax in the moment of death. I rose from ancient culture to magic, to art, to teenage ritual and back again.

Rock music had already created a connection with ritual, with sex, with role playing, and black metal took that ritual all the way back to its roots. Or all the way back to its body, at least, if the male teenage body could be called the *root*. In 1997 I'm too late and the wrong gender for being part of black metal, but I get to take part in the aesthetics and the performance: the makeup, the images, the parties. I get to join the white party that is the South, Norway, Scandinavia, the white taciturn gruel, and the vaults of silence.

Black metal and I emerge from this whiteness, in the silent *h*'s, those that cover complete darkness, total misanthropy, a complete and devouring black hole that gorges its way down and into the Norwegian roots. Perhaps black metallers in '91, '87, '93, like me in 2002, desire a black sheet to write on. Angry, lonely boys, looking for their own negative and a way to redefine the term *evil*. One winter they decide that everything should be black, the colour of evil, white upside down. When summer comes they decide to stop washing their hair, because the opposite of white is dirty. It's unclear whether or not they start to stink of rotten milk and wet dog. The next summer people start dying. At that point I'm still a long way from discovering the subculture, and when I become part of the scene six or seven years later, it's been cut up, jailed and convicted, become exalted and legendary.

But imagine what could have happened in '91, '93, '98. Imagine if churches hadn't needed to be burned down or gravestones toppled, but instead black metallers had reconsidered the craft and the traditions. Imagine if they had broken into churches and redecorated them to make spaceships, radical pirate radio studios and queer clubs . . . or maybe dropped a glitter bomb. Instead, the churches were set ablaze. A burning cross is a powerful cross. Crusading men have already planted them all over what we call history. Metal has become legendary; it gets press time and everyone is scared, it becomes tabloid and stripped of imagination. It becomes self-expression for insecure men who want to return to a time where they could have been strong. It concerns itself with mainstream values like dominance and control, it becomes monstrous, it simplifies, it's a tour de force and a power demonstration; it doesn't concern itself with critique. And no one questions the hate. Hatred is just an expression of strength. No one asks why the word *hate* actually has an audible h.

Black, we're taught in school, isn't a dynamic colour; it isn't a colour at all. It's just understood as the opposite of white. And it can't go anywhere. We can't hate. But I hate.

Can't we move? Or do we just avoid going there?

Black metal hated too; it dug itself further in as the '90s progressed, and opened up the underground to reveal something difficult and dangerous, but with the metallers' blind, boyish mythological fascination it grew paler and paler, whiter and whiter. The epic drama, the hierarchy, the gender segregation, the authoritarianism, the xenophobia, the silence, became its defining elements – all the things that already define society. In college in 1997 black metallers don't look different from neo-Nazis, and neo-Nazis don't look different from black metallers, and no one knows exactly who to beat up. The only people who keep their heads on straight are the brightly coloured Jesus kids, who spend all their time praying for everyone, since upside-down crosses and Nazi violence are the same in their dramatic staging of the fight between God and hell. The battle unifies them, Nazism and black metal and Jesus Revolution, so that everyone is a player in the eternal battle between good and evil, in which individuals dominate thanks to their faith or their race, or their misanthropy, and look down on the sheeple who accept so-called secular social democracy. A fucking party banquet of Southern knights.

A few years later the neo-Nazis have grown up, and returned to the Free Church congregations during the Aryan surge to the right. Black metal is mainstream and America has awoken. Then the porridge is complete: metal knights are regular knights, copied from a subculture into the mainstream, from subversive recordings and misanthropy to big-budget cinema productions about Norwegian resistance during the Nazi occupation, or about postwar expeditions, films like *Max Manus*, *The Battle for Heavy Water*, and *Kon-Tiki*. We're back where we started, outside Arendal, on Arne Myrdal's lawn with the People's Movement Against Immigration. We're all Southerners now.

Why does resistance always end up just polishing the traditions? Terese asks.

Or making way for them.

Good question, I say, or maybe Venke says. None of us, not even Terese, has a good answer.

From the beginning black metal is just a blackened and dirty version of pre-existing society, its growling an attempt to express a long strain of spoken, silent HHHHHHHHHHHHHHHHHHHHHs, collected from endless appearances of the word white. Every battle is linguistic.

We're able to see it differently now, twenty-five years after the golden era. We can say that early black metal is a modern version of Munch's paintings, lo-fi visions of the Norwegian anxiety about death and art, a negative of ourselves that only shows us our reflection. My face in black-and-white death, constantly pointed out by people as I walk through the loathed streets of Grimstad and Arendal, is a modern *Scream*.

The comments are usually:

CLEAN THAT UP

Or

YOU'LL NEVER GET MARRIED WITH THAT MAKEUP / THOSE CLOTHES / THAT HAIR

or

GIVE US A SMILE, THEN, DON'T BE SO GRUMPY

The boys in the metal band I'm in, and the punk boys and the rave boys, all get beat up in turns by the steroid-fuelled body-builders at the Arendal bus station. They leave me alone, I'm not threatening anyone's manhood, but I'm the one getting the predictions, the judgement, thrown at me. No one asks why I hate, no one uses that word, they call me *grumpy*, not even angry, but *grumpy*, six letters, something inconsequential and self-inflicted, something powerless, insignificant, something small in a small person, not something that's about society, or about them, just something that means I'm ruining things for myself, something that's in the way of my potential as an object.

We're on our way to the concert venue now. It's as if we have to open up the black again, and the music, to inject potential once more, and to add *and*?

Where is God?

In college I discover God in the mouth. He's hidden between the lips of the Christian girls, and not just in the muted words and the silent *h*'s. God is a musical presence. He's found in the heavy diphthongs and vowel sounds of the Southern accent, in their slow-paced speech and taciturn nature, in the vibrato that dominates the gospel choir's hymns.

In the breaks between psalms I hear smiles and chewing. The entire choir is always chewing gum. Their chewing-gum breath is mild and sacred, clean and minty. It's the corpse paint of the breath, I think. Something synthetic, white and clean to cover the human face. The little chemical wad of plastic and sorbitol that they chew is polished into a pearl in those soft and wet purgatories. They chew as if they've regurgitated it as cud, but they never swallow. Gum controls the mouth, stops it from speaking out of turn, but keeps it active, sensual. The gum is a reminder of life, a reminder of what the pulse, the tongue and the teeth really desire. The sound doesn't stop; like a beat it's always there; it becomes the sound of eternity. It, if anything, is God.

I curse the voice, the gum and the whole mouth, at home in my Southern witch's den. The school and the Christians try their best to control the mouth: through compulsory recitals of the Lord's Prayer, psalms (1989–92) and speaking in tongues, bans on swearing, and worried conversations about the faithless, hell and the devil (1996–99). My whole upbringing condenses into one question: How do you pray without faith?

The only thing I value in my mouth is spit. Hatred spits, scorns, and finally becomes bulimic. Something happens in my throat: a spiritual retching. Throughout my childhood I feel like I'm being sick without the nausea. As if that's how I talk and sing. I sense it in my dreams, walking to school, on the school bus. Under my desk every morning, like a glowing malpaís, is an oozing pool of black biblical sick.

At home, hidden behind black velvet curtains, I'm saved by the blasphemous material on my computer. I rush through Sacher-Masoch's *Venus in Furs* and Bataille's *Story of the Eye*, on the uncensored and unfinished '90s internet, and behind them I see my face mirrored on the computer screen. I scroll through eye and egg fetishes and voyeuristic fantasies, and in my own head I rename Bataille's novella *Story of the Throat*, a translation I lick and gnaw until I can feel something other than God's retching in my own throat. To do this, my throat has to become blasphemous. From my first year in primary school I spit out every school word contemptuously: When we sing psalms I harmonise off-key, adding evil resonances with my voice. The devil is always angry, and I'm always angry, I'm told, and that's why I allow myself to sing off-key. The devil and I are always a quartertone over or a semitone under, I think, and I rub myself against the rituals, swallow them, polish them with spit and regurgitate them. But when I use my voice for blasphemy, I do it with pleasure. The malpaís oozes in ornate patterns. Look at me, I'm gushing, it doesn't stop, but continues to drip down my desk, to the floor and down the drains in locker rooms, down to the underworld that supports us.

For the longest time I'm unable to understand what that feeling is. I can only feel it: the retching, the fear, the pleasure, and the overflowing. It's only years after I've left the witch's den and the classroom malpaís in exchange for a secular university in the capital, and long after I've repressed the feeling of God stuck in my throat, that I find the porn classic *Deep Throat* on an illegal peer-to-peer network, an awful low-resolution video. The file is so compressed, and all the moving genitals are so pixelated, that the film is practically censored and no longer fulfils its purpose. But it works for me. Early in the film the main character goes to see her doctor to ask why she can't orgasm. The doctor identifies the problem easily: her clit is actually in her throat. He is of course immediately willing to demonstrate how the issue could be solved. This part is less exciting to me. My kink is the idea that the throat is a site for happiness, as in the Art Garfunkel interview where he talks about the moment he realised that he could sing and calls it 'a feeling of happiness brought on by something that happened in my throat.' Linda Lovelace and Art Garfunkel, from kink to kink, blasphemy and happiness, it's all the same to me. Happiness is the throat that regurgitates God, as we clear that passage before we talk or sing, so that the throat can discover itself. In the throat's ecstasy, in the eroticism of the throat, the throat's hands are stretched out into the world. Out of the mouth gushes *and*?

I'm on my way home from practice with my first band in 1998. It's nearly summer and the sun scorches my black clothes and black hair. Black velvet sticks to arms, thighs and back as I dash through fields and housing estates and churchyards, past churches and parish centres with their crosses flying high and windows peering at me. When the wind blows through my clothes, I feel it's the Christian monuments sort of screaming at me. They know I'm the spawn of Satan. I'm a lonely black stain on the paper, one that isn't even allowed to battle the Jesus soldiers as a knight. With my band-practice confidence I curse them all.

From the top of a small hill, behind a few beeches and a thin white cross that wavers in the wind, comes the sound of voices. Each gust of wind ushers them toward me, and when the wind changes direction I almost can't hear them, until another word or phrase hits me in the face once more. The song is a psalm with lots of verses. Each phrase is stretched, the tones sustained, just as psalms are always sung, and within these sustained tones old women's voices quiver into each other. Each individual voice quivers, too, the way hats, tablecloths and the white cross quiver in an open-air church service. Deep inside these old women's throats their vocal cords vibrate against each other, body rubs against body, woodwork creaks against woodwork. Antiquated psalms, antiquated words, antiquated bodies, fossils united.

During this period in my life I scorn the vibrato. The Jesus girls have taught me that there's something Christian about the vibrato; there has to be, since they do it so much. In their boring gospel songs, the vibrato trills between God and the world, reflecting norms and rules. The most beautiful trill, if sung appropriately and in the most conventional way, is closest to God.

When I sing in my band, there's no vibrato, no sincerity, or depth. There's also no growl, HHHHHHH, I don't understand why that's the direction you're supposed to go, either. But deep down I'm actually tired of the metal conventions. Everyone in my circle missed the beginnings of black metal; it's been five years since all the action went down, and now everyone plays doom, a slower version with a more romantic outlook. In that genre, the bands shroud everything in a beautiful veil of dictionary English. None of us understands all the words, but on paper they look complex and ornamental. The clothes I should be buying are Victorian dresses and corsets, props from a time even more conservative than the dress code at the parish centres. No one actually questions anything. No one's really trying to rouse anything. Nor am I, except when I'm alone in the witch's dorm, and then I'm under the covers with my clit in my throat, cursing all the villages around me – Fevik and Rykene and Songe, and especially Saron's Valley – and all the radical evangelists. If it's really true that singing and writing can transgress the borders between the real world and someplace else, then there's no point in wrapping it all up in convention and corsets. Why should you not question, not doubt or go forth in chaos, not scream or bark or howl? You have to open up to the strange. You have to say something new.

I stay and listen to the parish choir at the top of the hill while I take off my jacket and jumper. I've been taught that song is a sacrament; it makes the holy words and the holy being real through the body. The same thing happens at band practice and when I curse, too, I take the words I and the others have written, preferably about denying god, about grief and hopelessness, and make them real. Composing a beautiful melody for the words *I hate God* excites me, but I don't dare sing it in front of the boys in the band: it sounds too primitive, too ecstatic. It's still better to let them find the lyrics, deep in their dictionaries.

The old women at the top of the hill lend their frail existence to the words that they find holy. The purity of the words and the physical entities of the voices melt together. It's a deeply Christian, almost Catholic moment, where faith is reified through its own complex, deeply sexual, religious melding. But it's the words, not Christ's blood and body, that manifest as they pass through the larynx, vocal cords and mouth. It's the faith, the story, that's reified. The trees, wind and the whole landscape curves around them. Below them, in the churchyard where we'll shoot our band photos later that same year, where I pretend to be crucified, is the underground, mile after mile of blood.

Perhaps art and magic are synonymous. Ever since someone worked out that a sound could be a word, or that you could draw an object. When signs, or words, emerged, you could describe the surrounding world, signless until then. And from there, figuring out that this language could also describe things that *don't* exist in the world was no great leap. It's possible to just make stuff up, take ourselves places we didn't know existed and that perhaps don't exist, that emerge only in the moment the voice, and later the reader or writer, is connected to language.

When this spell, language, is used to create gods and mythology, the fiction becomes so complex and self-referential that in fact it seems real, perhaps even self-aware. That might actually be what the singers in the old parish choir dream of: making God real through song, through their own real bodies, although they themselves of course would say that God is already real, that he exists. (And when they say that, he appears to them, in words.)

In ancient scriptures, and in everything written ever since, witches and magic have been a philosophical problem that stares God right in the eye. The witch's artistic expression is of course witchcraft, but just like the priests and the establishment, she uses both the body and words to give the craft life. The threat becomes real because these processes are similar, or perhaps, when all is said and done, *magic* is just a better word for God, faith, words and the existence of God. Perhaps it's this fear that makes my college class cross themselves when I exclaim *fucking hell* while our class photo is being taken, or maybe it's this fear that drove the writer of *Malleus Maleficarum*,

The Hammer of Witches, to include such an infinite number of pages with extrapolations of witch characteristics. Page after page filled with descriptions of how a witch uses words, body, and ritual, systematically eradicate her human and womanly qualities: her genitals are a dry desert that cannot reproduce; her throat is a broken connection between voice and body. Her body can be dressed in tempting animal- or humanlike disguises, and her voice is an artificial, sickly-sweet additive that tempts us to drink from the poisoned cup. The heavens open and God's holy presence is realised in the bodies of God-fearing people through their songs and sacraments, but the body of the witch, through her magical rituals, opens a parallel forbidden reality, underground, that doesn't belong in reality and *shouldn't* exist.

Language is transgressive, in both magic and religion. But in my world, when I say *fucking hell* in 1998, *magic* is the more appropriate word. The phrase is like a microscopic portal in a network between two worlds, and when I raise my voice I connect myself and the whole classroom to it. When I get told off and am given a written warning, the South reclaims ownership over language, the uncontrolled portal.

But that moment I say *fucking hell*, it isn't just the words but also the voice that Southern piety fears. The voice is uncontrollable. You can't even close your ears. Even though it's the word, *hell*, the name, that's supposed to conjure the devil into the material world, it's really the voice that calls and lures him. It's the voice that materialises and reproduces. It's the voice that acts, that shapes, that performs and expresses.

It's the voice that makes the language specific, so that a word is no longer just a word, but an exact moment. Like music, Southern witchcraft is more powerful than both God and Jesus combined.

So, I was too young to be part of black metal, and Venke and Terese weren't in on it, either. Maybe you missed it, too. But now we're a band, and the band has to play gigs. This gig has already started; we're on our way; this time what's oozing down and out onto the streets is *us*, through the parks and the squares. The audience has no idea we're performing, but you'll all hear it if you plug your ears and listen to your brain buzzing away. It's still not very distinct, but it's as though the brain sound has an additional echo. A slow feed is building in there, *Scream* backward, *corpse paint* in your ear.

We glide through town alongside the dragging drone of the trams, creaking and flowing onward like slow Viking ships, disappearing down Oslo's slippery throat. No one can see us: we've smeared hands and face with black henbane, rosemary and boiled plums, and now we blend into the shadows with the spirits and the 4G network.

Dusk falls while the tram slinks towards central Oslo. In the carriage, small patches begin to darken on empty seats, like grey dew; the stains grow steadily darker, as if daylight disappears faster there than the other spots, as if the streetlights don't work on them. It's us. The other, ordinary people don't see us; they just know that the seats we're sitting on are taken. We're the only ones who are able to make each other out, gradually, each other's shadows.

Two shadows recognise each other and high five. Random passers-by give a start; they hear the sound but don't see the hands.

As we get off the tram the trash-stench is under our noses, and under our feet, like glassy ideological ice. Inside the gate to the little townhouse flat where we're headed, the roots hiss under the lawn. We hear them, and we hear a faint rumble from the sound system inside the club: the sound of black. The windows are boarded up and painted shut, and the music emerges from deep in the middle of the building, frequencies oozing from every crack, a blurred unyielding mass, as if dough were rising in there.

Inside, the gig has already started; just like outside, it has always been under way. I hum along to the frequencies leaking out of the building into the backyard as we draw closer to the venue, through door after door, down hallways and into rooms. My voice changes as the sound gets louder and fills my ears more and more, changes to balance mouth and ears, impression and expression. After so much childhood biblical sick, my mouth is empty and dry, so much more room for *and?*

Now we're in the room where the gig is happening; some are on stage and some down on the floor. Everyone is dancing around slowly. We join, become part of the mass, on the floor at first and then the floor is elevated: we're on the stage. The music is slow, like the sound of a spinning ouroboros, a tail-eating drone that never started and never stops. We pick up instruments; perhaps we take them from someone else or swap a guitar for a synth, because it's important that the music changes, that there aren't too many lonely solos or riffs. We pick up microphones.

We try to summon a different kind of song, one that doesn't have God in the mouth or in the content either. All noises from our bodies are helpless and awkward, but through microphones and the strained sound system we don't sound real anyway. Our voices are coming from a synthetic body, from wires and metal threads and magnet capsules, but also from our bodies which have understood how veins can be wires that tear loose and rewire, bodies where the sound's new connections have already happened.

At times there are intervals in the concert and you can hear voices chatting quietly and familiarly. No one chews gum. Sometimes we nudge one another. Our lips move. Occasionally we burst out laughing. Then the playing begins again and the dancing continues; the faces and the bodies get redder and the expressions more intimate.

Some are making love to their own hand, or to someone else's hand. The clit is in the throats, in the hands, in the spit particles, on the lips and in the skin cells.

Who's who, no one knows. Someone has switched off significance and blacked out the dichotomies. Intimacy doesn't require hierarchies and formalities. Tonight we're both acquaintances and strangers. We can stand next to each other and feel the heat from each other's bodies; we can rub our hands against instruments or vocal chords against vocal chords; we can play, with or without instruments. Clothing fibres, skin, steel, plastic, rubber, bronze and tin from wires, instruments, and even *us*, all rubbing together, creating heat waves in the room. We dance on stage. We take each other's hands for brief moments, then let go again to continue to shake the instruments. The microphones are plugged into the underground electricity network and shock our skeletons. Our bones rattle inside us and next to us. There are more and more of us, and our shadows are just as big and real as we are. They are also strangers, they are also shadows and silhouettes, just like the round lamps on the walls and the stage light and the pegs and the dark stains in the woodwork on the walls, and the walls in the next room outside, and the next one after that, and the holes in the brick walls all the way out to the apartment building, and the hissing roots down there under the grass lawn. Everything comes together in moving lumps of dancing drone people and floating constituent parts, a cross-section of the constituent parts of the universe, a bubbling witch's cauldron.

Here we're strangers together, and we can replenish ourselves. It's important that we can be strangers together here, because outside we are the strangers. I was always strange, to the Christian girls and to the metal boys; strangers are those who ask where God is, or if what you just said about Satanism isn't actually similar to something in the Bible, or Doesn't your makeup look a bit like the ISIS flag, because black and white is always reminiscent of black and white, and text is always reminiscent of text, just as you can look yourself in the mirror and discover that your eyes look like the eyes of someone you don't like, someone you hate, someone who murdered someone, and whose picture you saw in the paper. Likeness is evil, too, even when we think it doesn't belong to us, and evil is loneliness. Or is it community? Do we just not go there?

We're what always gets between you and what really matters; we, and our objections. We separate you from the world in its perfection with our little paths awash in black bile. Like a diagnosed illness, we keep that world, that paradise you're trying to talk about, at bay; we catch you at a terminal between language and the world. If God is in the mouth, we can teach you to spit, or to retch, to stretch out of yourself. We've been practicing our whole lives.

I take the girl from *Puberty* along to the gig, paint ear plugs in her ears so she won't be afraid. She's here, with Munch, *the original corpse paint.*

We dance our way back to *fucking hell* in 1998, to primary school's *Our Father who art in Hell,* to witch's dorms and obscene scribblings in *Good News* and *Pan.* Those moments are so intimate for us, our *pleasure domes,* that we bring that energy along, to the domain of the metal boys, to the evangelical pietistic kingdom of heaven, to the parish centres, to *Filadelfia* and *The Word of Life,* to the Jehovah's Witnesses, to Old Town Oslo in 1993, to the suburban knights in Switzerland in 1981. Inside the most sacred spaces, we tear down merch tables, altars and baptismal fonts; we defile Pentecostal tambourines, spike belts, spit and lick and get pissed on holy water. We unplug the jacks from guitars and synthesizers and shove them into every orifice, theirs and ours, connect us to them, into them, out of us. We're jacked up, we're plugged in, we're online, and we raise the gospel and rock microphones and start singing, maybe we sing the lyric *I hate God*, in piercing, electrified girl-choir voices, using all different melodies, intentionally or unintentionally. This, it seems, is just as ugly to the Christians as it is to the metallers.

The sound of the song is atonal, as if the bodies it surges through were analogue synthesizers that oscillate and vibrate, as if the sound were a pattern or web, as if our mouths were plugged into pipes and chords that rub and hiss at each other.

We're made of flesh and varying tempos: one for the muscles in our jaws when they gasp, one for impulses from the nerves that cause laughter, one for blood and one for the digestion of every individual substance that we have consumed. There's a tempo for cell division and the body's disintegration, because all this is happening inside the bodies, everything has always already begun, the gig is also life, the gig is death too. We stretch the web in different directions, we feel the PH value sway between alkaline and acidic. Between us and outside us, outside of cells and muscles and skin and everything we've been taught is our own form, is the room, or the beginning of it. The room begins at the point where we no longer recognise our own matter, where we begin to doubt ourselves. The room begins where only voices and menstrual blood and icy breath stretch out of us, and just where they stretch out of us and sort of look back at us, we start to doubt if we can actually claim that we *are* all the matter that exists within what we've been taught is our own form. Then the sweat follows; it, too, stretches out of us and into the room, and perhaps we sneeze, perhaps we cry, as more and more of our own bodily matter transforms itself from subject to world-tissue.

We stretch out of our own shapes and become space, with the breath, with the blood and the voice. Now we're in our own atmospheres, in our own cosmos, in the smallest big spaces, our own metaphysical matter.

The Pact

In an early version of the film I'm writing, the girl from *Puberty* is the main character in the story. She's travelling in a time machine from the 1890s, her own time, to our time. There she's going to look for Edvard Munch, to crush him, as revenge for painting her. In the story's opening we're told that Munch has already travelled through that same time machine, to pursue his dream of playing in a popular black metal band.

The plot wasn't my idea, but came from a conversation I had with Venke and Terese before a band practice. Maybe that's why I like it. It's a communal document, detached from the lonely writing process. The story, and the way we throw together ideas, reminds me of *Jubilee*, that punk film where Queen Elizabeth I is transported to an anarchist violent version of 1970s Britain, with punk icons playing the leads. Elizabeth surveys her ravaged kingdom before returning to her own time, and the film might just be implying that she should have taken Elizabeth II and the whole British Empire with her, the empire that created this imperialist pigsty of a modern society.

As the conversation about our film takes place, I enjoy daydreaming about how the end of the finished picture should play out. I see the *Puberty* girl killing Munch off in two steps.

First off, she'll video one of his band's gigs, and then she'll play the recording as she paints on the film. She'll mess up Munch's face by drawing cartoon sketches, doodles and cryptic speech bubbles on it, and then she'll draw infantile cocks hanging out of the mouths of the entire band. Finally she paints the whole image black. THE END.

That plot doesn't pan out. I'm not able to write anything more than quick summaries of our conversation, and I ram my head against the scenes in which the actual story is being told, this story that's supposed to go from A to B, from past to present, from character A to character B. The rules of realism in my head are far too strict, dictating how a 1890s character should react to being moved 130 years into the future, and when I sit down to write the scenes, my imagination halts. I can describe exactly, down to the most minute points, the moments when I stop and feel lonely, when the band and the bonds disappear and are replaced with writing rules from the university in New England, where my professor looms over me and tells the class that my submitted short story isn't credible, that it's just angry and messy, incoherent. Instead of raising my hand to say that Hemingway and Raymond Carver, and why not throw in Foster Wallace, are an insult to the brain, and ask where the women writers on the curriculum went, I write my next assignment as a satire of a Carver short story, the scene set in Norway and with a female protagonist, to make it as believable as possible. The teacher is impressed; he says I write as if it were me, but in a way that's universal, from the outside, with insight. From the outside, with insight: that's what the art of writing is, maybe all art, after the subjective structures and the subjective untethered imagination have been tamed, and when it isn't the canvas, the screen, the compendium sheets, or Edvard Munch's black metal band being painted black, but just my own seething hatred of the structures that are being erased by white.

Isn't that why the underground, the avant-garde, the B movies and comics and fanzines and black metal originally emerged: to be free of the consequences and this relentless comparison to reality, and to open up to other structures? To the crawling and creeping and hissing and noisy structures? They were able to create space for a different kind of art, a different kind of writing. Or maybe they just created a new set of rules, new hierarchies? Am I stretched between spaces I can't reach, that I don't feel entitled to step into? I have to keep looking for that place that I could call *writing*, that I could call the film.

Some scenes I can manage. I have no issue with scenes where characters die or disappear, scenes where shapes disappear or dissolve. I'm better at killing people off than I am at giving them life through character descriptions and realistic scenes in which people interact. Something seems to be getting in the way of the exposition, the description, this world that looks like reality.

Perhaps it's my thirst for revenge. Maybe I'm too vindictive to write anything from inside the structures, from the beginning, from the outside, with insight. Perhaps hatred does hamper writing, just as I've been told my whole life. Hatred isn't plot or continuity, says my creative writing teacher in my head, and hatred isn't a good motivation or intention, it's a tale too short and primitive to be told, it can't be the focus.

But that's the short version of the film: the only version. I just want to take revenge on film history, literary history, art history, paint the whole picture black, paint the whole screen black, force Microsoft Word to let me write in white on a black background. I just want to be allowed to hate, unrestrained. THE END.

I wasn't allowed to write that text at university in New England. The university, along with the whole art industry in that place, looked less like imagination and more like the South. In the South I never got to transcend genre and form, not in my essay assignments, and not in the classroom. I wasn't allowed to hate.

Hate is the only word that Christian and heathen Southerners react to equally powerfully. Hatred belongs to the devil and to the Second World War. Only Hitler and the German soldiers hated, and we're taught they're the only ones we can hate back. That's the one thing we've decided everyone here agrees on. And we never talk about it, sitting at our desks in the '90s, primary school, secondary school, college. First it's the fiftieth anniversary of the outbreak of World War II, then the fiftieth anniversary of VE Day. We make fried turnips as they did during the war, and we're taught about concentration camps, we're taught about mass suggestion, about manipulation, but we don't talk about hatred. Maybe hatred is magical, maybe the war will return if we begin to define it, differentiate it, dig out its significance, and find the sound.

Have you thought about how similar those words are: HATE and HOPE? Four letters, a voiced *h*, a quick, full vowel between two consonants. Maybe both words depend on those consonants to contain the energy, the rebellion, the reckoning, the infinity.

Have you thought about how good it feels to say that you hate? That deep *a*-sound: in Norwegian it's the mouth's most open vowel, the one that's pronounced entirely by a slack jaw, the tone the doctor asks for before instruments are stuck down your throat, or the last tone from the dying and the dead. The A emerges from the underground and the downfall.

Southerners say *hadår* or *hadær*, depending on how far south or west they are. It's even more magical than the English *hate*, softer, saltier, more sheltered and concealed, closer to the kingdom of the dead, *Hades*. This softer language stretches further down into the deep, into the sea, the underground; the magical dimensions.

In the draft of the film that's never written, the *Puberty* girl meets other subjects from other paintings. Together, after an eternity in stiffened oil paint, alone and objectified, the subjects plot art-terrorism. As I force myself to think through the narrative trajectory, the ordinary scenes, the girl's shock at the present day's violent expressions and technological development, the sequences where she searches for Munch, the scenes that are normal and real, the writing grinds to a halt. I sit hunched over my laptop screen and the empty text document, thinking about how broken objects can bond, and what kind of band could emerge among them. Sometimes I type in a lonely Å, to have something to look at, to talk to someone.

There are several reasons for my writer's block. The girl's anger at Munch reflects my own hatred of God and the world, of course. *Puberty* is me, the broken object–subject. If I keep writing this story, the writing won't be a different magical place, but a repetition, a well-behaved reproduction of a pre-existing narrative, set in Norway with a female main character, as if I'd once more just traced a pattern for good art. The film version only works as an idea, before it's fitted into the pattern. It's better as a smouldering flame, distilled to one sentence: *Girls hating through centuries*. THE END.

In Venke's flat, colloquially referred to as the witch's den, Venke is stretched out on the chaise-longue drawing graphic erotica. I'm seated by the fireplace typing in an Å or *girls hating through centuries, THE END*. Terese is time-lapsing sourdough loaves rising on the kitchen counter. A new, long conversation has been happening between us, over several days, and it continues every time we meet in the hallway. We discuss what's progressive, what could be subversive, why we care about it. What's the point of confronting anything at all in Norwegian society? Can art express rebellion in our time? It's been fifty years since performance art got explicit, and soon it'll be thirty years since the arrival of black metal, riot grrrl punk and *Gender Trouble*. If there's anything at all that might still have a subversive effect, says Venke, what would it be?

How would people today have reacted to all that performance art, those horror films and subcultures? asks Terese.

Perhaps by just ignoring it all, excluding it, quickly sweeping it under the rug, like they did to black metal before all the crime, I say.

Weren't the black metal bands actually still there, even after the murder and the arson? Terese replies.

That depends how you define black metal, Venke interjects.

And how you define 'excluded', I say.

Think about that word, EXCLUDED. To exclude something, to explain something. The nature of the subversive isn't actually to be directly visible but to roam the shadows, to give texture to the seemingly shiny and clean, to scrawl public walls with inexplicable nonsigns that refuse to materialise into language. The subversive desires to be seen and not seen simultaneously, it desires both to be excluded and to be explained. But it's so easily muted, left behind, forgotten, excluded without being explained. Or it gets picked up and transformed into a language we all understand, that is, explained, but for some reason that always seems to mean commercialised.

In 1991 you could, on the surface, ignore black metal and its subversive content. Norway was too secular to be shocked by upside-down crosses and guitar riffs without the usual muting of strings. It was as if they didn't exist, until murder and church arson existed: conventional crime, dangerous young men. That was a language that could be understood. Later, black metal music was commercialised, too. It was translated, adapted for sales, polished and tightened, giving it a more saleable image. When Varg Vikernes was imprisoned, society's idea of rehabilitation, the music lost that messy, fat-stained, insect-like buzzing, and was remastered into a more modern, healthy and powerful rock image. Man emerges from the gutter, transformed into the übermensch, again, as always. An understandable language. Crisp and crackling photocopier fanzines projected into the big and beautiful picture books of nostalgia.

The genuinely subversive is still untouched, the *h*s are still silent. What is it we're lacking if we, in art and in life, just repeat and repeat and repair and repair versions of ancient hierarchies and rituals? What do we exclude? Can you hear it? What is it we're still not saying?

Terese lowers her head until her ear rests on the kitchen table. She's filming one of the sourdoughs, one that has risen over the edge of the bread tin. It looks as if she's listening to something inside the woodwork. Venke is stretched out on the couch, arms dangling over the sides. If I photographed her now, she'd resemble a young Varg Vikernes, with that long hair and graceful posture. That image is far too romantic, nostalgic, adapted for sales. We paint it black. The death of art.

That's what I need to write. The death of art. That's the black screen. That's where we have to begin, where writing has to begin. It makes more sense to talk about art's potential if it's already dead. Total misanthropic black. With art-death we have the opportunity to see the significance of the resurrection we desire, the colourful text that's slowly typed and fed into the black screens, keeping time with the fermenting dough. The band searches for a resurrection. Maybe that's why the only scenes in my film that I'm able to write are the ones where someone dies or disappears. Maybe it's not just about God, and maybe hatred isn't about burning something to the ground, but about discovering a flame that illuminates the darkness, a match that ignites or creates something new.

This conversation has been carried on in band practices and knights' duels. But this afternoon it's more extensive. We look at each other, Terese with her ear to the kitchen counter, Venke with her head resting upside down on the couch, me through the laptop screen, and without a word, a pact is written in black misanthropic ink on a parchment of gurgling sourdough. I, we, start to see the contours of a future where we can dig up a few ghosts, find a few new and radical definitions of art, of relations, participation, creation. Maybe we have to kill off our entire definition of what art is. Because didn't art distinguish itself through separation of aesthetic practice from rituals, magic and revolt? Ritual, magic, people's revolts, they are the thick brush, the bad art.

We know that the band, and the symbiotic relationships we create, have to be centred. We know that's what people are looking for: *the relations, the symbiosis.* We want to experience them, and create them, see them swell and form between others. We want to study and act; we want to be actors and voyeurs. The goal has to be coming together, an artistic connection, ingredients that together make a brew. Is it at all possible to get close to people that way, or in any way? Was that how I was able to see you during the gig? Or was I? What does it mean to 'get close'?

Maybe this is what writing could be, too: a place for communal, creative rituals, instead of that lonely voice confined to a white text document. Am I actually lonely when I write? If I am, it's only according to that one definition of reality, the one that reproduces the subject in God's image, and so declares that I am alone, that I occupy the role of the solitary genius. Maybe writing could be redefined, so that it isn't a position but a search: I'm in search of community, and I search for that place where God isn't.

God isn't the one writing anymore; it's all the girls sitting inside paintings, hating. I'm looking for us.

THE END, for now. I put aside writing for a while, and we the band begin our search for ingredients for what we no longer call gigs but rituals. In this expanded band format we begin by studying *Malleus Maleficarum,* or *The Hammer of Witches'* notes on witch practice and the witch trials. But instead of looking at the arguments and the content of the descriptions, we study their tone and the sound, as if they were music. The descriptions are full of meticulous detail, of the witches' rituals and of society's – the torture and execution of witches. Crime and punishment are set to surprisingly similar tunes. The language looks like one long black metal text, Venke points out, and she's right, the sentences downright glisten with their own dark ecstasy. But the perspective is more specific, clearly punching down, delivered as dribbling phrases driven by misogyny and xenophobia; the bourdon notes of the dominant. This is patriarchy's own seething witch's cauldron. We dive below the surface and go deeper into the books to find what we are looking for, what concerns us.

The Hammer of Witches was digitised a long time ago and can be read on any screen in the world, but there are printed copies in existence, too; they're nestled deep in old library shelves. You could easily confuse these editions with other medieval manuscripts, but they differ from such books in one particular way. The paper's makeup, if examined through lenses and tested in a laboratory, would resemble a porn magazine more than your typical old manuscripts might, because of the conspicuous number of stains smudging the text. Some paragraphs are practically illegible; they feel rough to the fingertips and page after page sticks together. The chapters on punishment and torture are particularly difficult to decipher without having to resort to the digitised edition. The book has been subjected to some rigorous use over the centuries.

But no one has looked at these stains under a magnifying glass. The physical content of this book hasn't received the same depth of analysis as the textual – all those hundreds of pages of information and discussions concerning the nature of witchcraft, and crime and punishment. The confession and punishment scenes have attracted the most diligent attention and therefore have the stickiest paper. It's impossible to determine what the stains are composed of . . . if it's spilled wine, coffee, milk, sweat, or semen. Venke, Terese and I reckon it's the effluence of excited genitalia.

What is certain is that the stains are part of a conversation, a comment section that transgresses time, place and dimension. A stain is also an imprint, an imprint from one person's situation, something that stretches out of the body and is projected, involuntarily, into the future, where another body in another time, in another space, will open that same page and study the stain. We can pick up a print copy of *The Hammer*, and assume it contains traces of another reader's kinks, the mounting desire, the climax and that pathetic mortal dread that follows. The absorbent paper soaks up the body's signature, the musical notations of desire. The stains symbolise what the book itself describes with the utmost empathy and precision: *The Way Whereby a Formal Pact with Evil Is Made.*

Terese adds the book to her tablet, searches different words and discovers that *sperm* is mentioned a total of sixty times, appearing throughout the book. That feels like a disproportionate number, and at the same time, in light of the paper's consistency, completely fitting. Venke thinks that word searches and word counts could be our modern ingredients list. In which case, *The Hammer of Witches* would make for quite the interesting brew.

The text describes semen as a sacred fluid, unlike the filthy blood of menstruation. Semen is white, too: the sacred stains cover the black ink with white, layer on layer, exceeding the paper's capacity for absorption. A whiteout of witchcraft, like a form of social cleansing, an erasure.

The book repeatedly describes how the inability of devils and witches to reproduce has been verified, and that they instead collect men's sperm to create perverted demon children. Those who might threaten the balance of power in society are often described as sperm collectors. Europeans were referred to as such when they began to infiltrate the portside brothels of Nagasaki and other Japanese cities. When Europeans appear in *shunga*, Japanese erotic art, they are frequently, and strikingly, shown collecting sexual juices in cups and other containers. Witches' brew.

Witches are sperm collectors, then, according to *The Hammer*, which does not know that its very own pages have performed the same task. In an attempt to pinpoint what witchcraft is, the book itself becomes a blasphemous document.

It's impossible to predict what the effect might be if we were to rip out the most porous pages of the book, crumble them into the witch's cauldron over a low heat, and then drink a nice cup of tea from the brew. But that's what we have to do to create our own rituals. And so we sign our own formal pact, in blasphemy with each other. We enter into a magical triangle: a satanic community, spawn of Satan.

It's been a few months. I've completely abandoned the idea about Munch joining a band and the *Puberty* revenge scenario. I've put the disk with the film file in a drawer. Instead, I study rituals. I'm sitting in the witches' den watching Otto Muehl's therapy scenes in the film *Sweet Movie* over and over again. The scenes depict Muehl's real-life Friedrichshof commune, in what is obviously the mid-1970s. Everyone eating together around a table. It feels like a party. People play with their food. Its consumption looks like a revolutionary ravaging dance. Then the members of the commune start throwing up, at first a little hesitantly, and then with practised professionalism, their fingers digging the food out from deep down in their throats. When they're done, they start shitting, as if they've been digging further and further into themselves, further down, inside the body, downwards through the chakras, all the way to the deepest and dirtiest, the most frightening and perhaps also the most human. In the end a few of them sit in a ritual circle, shitting on their plates. The other participants watch and cheer them on, and later they honour the faeces, dancing with full plates of excrement and offering the contents to each other and to the camera. As a finale they smear the skin of one participant with shit, then smear several more. They smear each other's outsides with each other's insides.

The poo ritual is a version of *HHHHH*, a display (and total transgression) of everything that was silenced or repressed in postwar Austria. I recognise it; it's the biblical sick, a catharsis of repressed social democracy. The commune delights in society's most private waste. It's social critique in the form of an attempt at a parallel utopian society that lives out both primal desires and revolutionary artistic visions. Through performing these forbidden, primitive actions, the commune tries to do something creative with the dark-brown colour that the Austrian (and European) postwar era had repressed as deeply as possible and never reckoned with: fascism.

Sweet Movie's main character, Miss Canada, winds up in the commune after a series of degradations. At the start of the film she is crowned the most innocent girl in the world. The competition is a beauty pageant in which girls from different countries spread their legs before a vagina inspector. When Miss Canada lies down in the gynaecologist's chair and spreads her legs, an almost sacred light beams from her cunt, a light that these days would remind you of a laptop opening ('. . . and then there was light'). After winning the competition, the innocent girl experiences a series of humiliating sexual encounters, representing her deep submergence in the buried trauma of postwar Europe. And now she's here with us, a spectator to the faeces ritual.

The first time I saw the film, watching the ritual was dark and horrifying. It was a descent into hell, total chaos. It's a much more violent assault on the senses than misanthropic black metal.

Rewatching the film now, I'm not as frightened and I can understand what's cheerful about the shit ritual, that destructive energy in actions that transgress and mock all boundaries. We're far from *The Hammer*'s consequences for ritual transgression; punishment and torture have been replaced with excitement and banter. But I also see the structures within this so-called complete transgression. I see Otto Muehl, the alpha male who reigns over this highly hierarchical commune. I know about the abuse that grows from this hierarchy; I see the evil in the attempt to transform a single artist's vision into genuine collective self-expression. I see a tribute to patriarchy and capitalism, because they're paying tribute to production, albeit a primitive production, but capitalism is after all already primitive. In the end we're all producers, dreadfully productive ones, too, and there's nothing capitalism loves more than productivity, eternally accelerating and ever more efficient production. Shit is the root of capitalism. The Friedrichshof commune has traced productivity right down to its roots, to the faeces, and as a result the ritual only loops back to the same Austria that they want to transcend. I see social control, I see capitalism, I see patriarchy, I see God.

The scenes that follow are the last we see of Miss Canada. She's in a mud bath, performing movements that verge on erotic dance. Her whole body, apart from her eyes, is smeared with Europe's brown mass. She spreads her legs, but there's nothing between them, no laptop light and no genitalia, only brown thick mass. This scene is beautiful: Miss Canada has lost her own form, she's part of the mud, she lives in a space filled up with a brown, shapeless substance.

I want someone to melt or disappear like that in my film too, like Miss Canada in the brown mud. But instead of first degrading them, I just want them to appear and disappear. And I want the agent to be black. Black is my colour, the colour of the Norwegian underground; brown is too similar to Austria, too Central European. It's darker up here, smoother, quieter. I picture something that corrodes into black and disappears; perhaps we'll all be digitised and I can live entirely online, or maybe it will be a more straightforward corporeal death. Perhaps the black fluid is coming from the body itself: the gall oozes from people; the insides take over, destroying the outside, our subversive components give us a texture that we didn't know we had, but not with something we produce, just something that's always there, something we don't feel. Something that exists, shapeless, inside us, like blood, because we can't stab our blood and feel pain. This blackness should disintegrate us. In the end we'll look like little foetuses, and then we're gone. THE END.

Maybe the only way an artist can escape capitalism and patriarchy today is to use art to disappear as an individual. The artists must completely wash away their person and self-expression, along with their individual characteristics and even their own imprint, their own life in the physical world. The artist's person, ego and even body must disappear quite literally into gunk, shit and black bodily waste. That's where something new can start.

I won't be able to write this, but I'll try. I want writing that can summon death, that can summon the disintegration of human tissue. The tissue melts in a chemical, or magical, or alchemical reaction. I don't desire total freedom, or total misanthropy. Do you get that? I desire magic, the same alchemical reaction that transforms hatred to a new or strange form of love.

That might be why I'm writing this to you. I need someone to write to, someone else, someone who isn't here and who I'm pulled toward. This yearning for you is a yearning for the unknown, the unwritten; the impossible place. Like the love reflected in the death scene I want to write in the film, or the love in a collective suicide. What sort of love is this? Self-sacrificial love in its furthest extension? Or is it love of the object, art, self-destruction? The destruction of our incomplete interpretations of relationships, life and death, you and me?

Where the writing is going, and where Venke, Terese and I are headed, I don't know yet. But I wanted to write to you. I just feel like I've gotten closer to you now. Am I crazy?

I rummage through the bile gunk, that gelatinous black background, with my little white letters. I find something in there, little blind bits. I'm getting closer to something. Intimacy. Love through murder, writing that kills, fusion. Do I write people to death to get closer?

I write a satanic pact between you and me. THE END.

Rituals

As I type in *I write a satanic pact between you and me* . . . in the email application, the word I is corrected to AI by the automatic spell check. Representation and subject are switched. In the future there are no boundaries. YOU could be UUE, or maybe that O could stretch a little further, into the magical DOC or DOCX of the text. ME could be MPEG or MP4, the same file format as the black metal bonus material, the same format that my film will become in the end. The transformation and magic have already begun, the formats converted to rituals around us.

Let's all zoom out a little, and turn the camera to face out. We're on a street. It's dark, it has to be night. The wind howls. The beams from the scattered street lamps don't reach each other, and we are in the dark spot between two lit stretches. Further up we can see the branches of a tall birch sway in the wind, but around us it's dark, as if we have to see through darkness to get to the light. The here and now is blackened. It has been rubbed out, or doesn't exist for us. But the future, over there, that we can see. Behind the swaying branches we see the contours of a building. Slowly we close in on the light.

The building in front of us looks familiar, the colour, the contours, it's got to be the old Munch museum, but as we move closer, time gradually picks up its pace. This has to be 2019, so the paintings have been packed up and moved to their new home in Bjørvika, and now it's closed, it's probably 2020, and the new museum will have opened a long time ago. By the time we get to Sirkus Square, several more years must have past, and the old building in Tøyen collapses, paint flaking.

Slowly, culture is transformed back into nature. The building's white halls and the cloakroom's warm yellow hues fade, as if the paintings were what held the walls and the pigments together. The museum rooms have become set pieces in a story that's finished, a reality that's no longer real. The metal detectors remain, continuing to scan their own machinery, and the cameras in the corners film nothing so many times over that the image creates its own feedback loop.

This is where I'm writing, in the abandoned museum. Munch's bonus material.

When we push open the old glass doors, the building lets out a sigh, as if we've opened a bottle of sparkling water.

'Munch burp,' says Terese. She's at the front and got a gust of musty air directly in her face.

Venke sniffs through the opening, yells HELLO! and wriggles her way through the crack we've made.

The echo travels around the empty exhibition rooms before it seeps back out again, toward us.

It's quiet in there for a little while.

Venke, I whisper, to no response.

Then the sound of a machine starting up is heard from the far end of the room.

We're sneaking in through the crack now, Terese and I, along with all the others who have begun to follow us. The rumour has clearly spread. The conclave expands. The future is caught up and devoured by the present, the image moves back and forth.

In the biggest hall the rain trickles down the walls from rot-holes in the ceiling. There are still marks from the biggest paintings. *The Researchers* used to hang here, the painting with Mother Earth sitting nursing in the middle, with an edging of children's bodies, all joined together, surveying the sheep-backed rocks in the background. 'She provides the milk of science', Munch is supposed to have said about the female figure in the middle. If you squint at the middle of the imprint left by the painting, you see the water collect into large falling droplets, stained golden white by chemical pus, environmental toxins and old paint, as if there were still an engorged breast where the art once was.

Terese and Venke immediately begin working on the wall, redirecting the water-milk in formations across an imagined canvas, like a little water carousel that slowly paints its own artwork. A couple of other artists have started painting abstract motifs directly onto one of the other walls in blood-red. Their hands drip with the blood, which drips from our eyes too if we get too close.

In the middle of the room is an oblong machine. At over two metres long, it's like a small train carriage. Two people are operating it from a panel on one side, twisting and turning oversized buttons and levers. Solid fasteners hold together a large steel plate that stretches out into a short tray on the other end. It looks like an enormous, old-fashioned Geiger counter or some sort of nuclear energy research device from the Los Alamos laboratory in America, but it's an old 3D printer. The operators gently nudge it. The machine coughs a little and the rear end is raised and then opens slightly to let out the cough.

'Is everyone here?' asks one operator.

There are quite a lot of people in the room now, maybe twenty or thirty. I recognise a few of them. Only I and a couple of others are standing around the machine; the rest are busy creating and hanging their own artwork.

'What are you making?' I ask.

'It's not that easy,' says an older woman with her arms crossed.

The printer is too old to follow instructions. It was made before they really got the hang of the technology, and age has left it both enchanted and inebriated. It doesn't produce the programmed results. But maybe it can show us something we've secretly wished for, made from recyclable plastic packaging. Behind the operators are several black bags, bursting with trash off the streets. I exhale, relieved. I just remembered the mill at the bottom of the sea and hope no one asks for herrings and gruel.

Something's being printed right now. It takes a long time, almost an hour, and the machine occasionally huffs and puffs, like a dying Dot Matrix that has to be repaired and rebooted over and over again. Finally, something is spat out of the metallic colon: an almost living 3D baby.

One of the operators picks up the baby, in that way you do, scratches it a little under the chin, cradles it and carries it over to the other operator, who looks sceptical but also a little impressed.

Did anyone think about this?

No one answers.

The plastic mould is still warm, she says.

The figure is passed around. The quality's poor. Messy dimensions and with plastic residue hanging from the ends of toes, lips and skull; but it still looks lifelike, and it's warm, like a living body, though rapidly cooling.

Venke and Terese's milk painting is completely soaked, and shapes have started to appear in it, a breast, or an udder, or perhaps that's a poison gland on the canvas. Under the image, in big red letters, they've written: *Suck on me.*

Throughout the day, the printer continues to spit up human-like figures, at first warm and soft, then hard and cold. We hang them around the room, and begin increasingly to wander about, as if we're now an audience at our own exhibition.

In a moment one of the operators has grasped the first art baby's head and torn the figure off the wall, swinging it around. The rest of us start to do the same. I grab a slightly larger plastic baby and begin swinging it around by its legs; round and round until the head takes flight and hits a wall and the shoddy plastic cracks.

A gasp ripples through the room. Our movements take on a forced harmony before we carry on with our separate activities. For a brief moment the norms have surfaced, the South, or whatever we're calling it now, in us, even in here, in the future museum. We've gone too far. A reaction is provoked. The plastic babies ask: Should art that depicts children's figures have different values, different ways of communicating with reality than other images, even when they're created from plastic or animated lines? Should we be allowed to be a picture? ask the babies. Should we ignore the formats, shouldn't JPEG or MPEG or RAW or TIFF exist, so we look straight at a subject that isn't there? Should there be chips and pieces and holes in us that aren't permitted to be art and fantasy?

In that brief moment of hesitation, we're caught between art's conservative ideas about the independence of the artistic genius, and a moral understanding of reality as a place where some ideas are not permitted to be imagined, even though the imagination exists; even though, for us, it could have been something else, given us something, created something. This is also where *Puberty* is positioned. Not just in the rift between child and adult, but between Munch's canonised genius and the exploited girl who models for him, either literally or figuratively. Can we save her without being accused of destroying art, I wonder, but here she is, in the middle of the scene, with every right: the right to hate, the right to destroy. She has almost ripped off her own head, slipped on a BDM-format animated teenage head that resembles her, and started headbanging.

And then the rest of us move on, too. I continue to twist the plastic fibres with my hands, skin and meat and bone cells. The hatred, the rights of the artistic geniuses, and of their objects, swirl around the girl in the room. Here, all formats are transformed. Here there's no collective shame of association. Here is BA (binary archive), and BAR (horizontal bar menu object file) and BB (database backup). We're here, in this impossible place. The place God can't see. We feel him searching for us though, for a brief moment.

114

Art attacks itself. The exhibition is constructed, then destroyed again. We tear down the paintings. We wade through the blood paint. It's streaming from our eyes. The entire house headbangs.

Then the ritual ends. We start to zoom in again, back to our own time and our own witches' dens, but as we reel back, we throw the art babies back into the machine. The children and the teenagers, now completely cold, completely hardened, cracked and broken. The printer has become increasingly alert throughout the day, and now it is really up to speed. It shreds the plastic moulds almost immediately, then reshapes and rechristens them. As the room expands and the details are erased in the distance, we watch it spit out the first victim of the shredding, an ugly IKEA vase, narrow and hollow, of the TAJT variation. A Scandinavian reproduction monster.

Let's rest in the side panel briefly, before we return to reality. You and me.

Some rituals don't need to be performed or written out properly. They can, for example, be written as lists.

MAGICAL SCULPTURE PARK SCULPTURES
1. Venke can be seen embracing a Rodin figure.
2. Terese is deep inside Dan Graham's chamber.
3. I lick the bedrock alongside Jenny Holzer's letters.
4. Everyone squats pissing around Ann-Sofi Sidén's *Fideicommissum*.

And another list

HOW I'M GOING TO KILL GOD

has no content at all. It's so pathetic.

Sometimes, after working through the night, we sit tired and half naked on our beds, in pants and maybe only a T-shirt, in a pose that resembles *Puberty* but without the shame. And then something has begun. A new ritual. Without anything really starting. A ritual is a feeling, a band feeling, a sensation of the bonds that tighten into eternity knots and squeeze us together, not uncomfortably, just closer, so we feel the radioactivity in our bodies and are bound to each other.

No one can see into the room; no one can spot us, photograph us, stream or paint us. The blinds are drawn for the people who sometimes smoke in the backyard, piss behind the corner or come to argue with someone on the phone. We're not sexy, either, sitting on our beds in our underwear. For some reason it's important to me to make that clear. Maybe because I don't want you to see; the gaze on the naked body is so difficult. Picture us as containers, as meat and minerals and fluids, like bags: an outside made of leather, pockets in several places, and with contents of soft and hard body tissue, held up and in by a series of mathematical figures and fluid-based transport systems. Think of us as stage curtains, leaking yellow, red and blue light, and smoke from smoke machines, from every curtain edge. Picture it. That in itself is a ritual. I'm writing this to you.

One of us has blood on her hands, fumbling a little with her crotch. She says: You know when you insert a tampon and it's stuck sort of diagonally, like that? and points with a bloody finger. As if our insides always changed form, and the vagina always swallowed tampons and menstrual cups a little differently. We disappear toward the back of the room, to a toilet, and continue our discussion from there, in the background. *Puberty*, I'm writing her into the ritual, joins us there. From the bathroom we're heard but not seen: only our shadows are visible. We talk about cups and vacuums and how they're like leeches, sucking their way up the crotch, as we lift up nightgowns, pull down pants and use twigs to rub ourselves with black henbane.

Someone has smeared blood over her thighs, and one of us gets it on her face. We begin applying makeup around the bloodstains, adding more colours, initially just on her face, then on everyone's. One of us is painted in a black-metal style, but using green instead of black, and adding glitter. *Puberty* is painted across Edvard Munch's *Self Portrait on the Glass Veranda*, blood all over the face with thick aquamarine lines. That seems appropriate, says Terese.

Black henbane doesn't burn the skin, on the inside or outside; it just warms, rubs, accentuates the shapes of our orifices like glowing rings. Behind us our shadows are long, moving in increasingly dark circles, like our own feedback loop. The dimensions open up, more rings slide up inside our bodies, through the uterus. We're no longer Scandinavian reproduction blueprints. The rings twist around the bones in our spines, until we exhale them like smoke rings, respire them. Then they rise, across town, ring 1, ring 2, ring 3, ring on into the cosmos.

Maybe we rise, too. Maybe we half carry each other, half float? Maybe we sit on the twigs and use them to float, like brooms.

Or wait, maybe the twigs are brushes and we use them to paint the floor and the walls, or ourselves. Maybe the twigs are instruments, or microphones that we attach to ourselves.

Being a witch doesn't need to be more difficult than that. Just look: Venke lifts her hair with one hand, holding two twigs in the other. She uses the twigs to cut off a big lock of hair, as if they transformed into scissors on their way to her head, turning back into twigs afterwards. As Venke cuts, the clipped hairs are immediately transformed into spaghetti. Where the hair was cut it grows out again; the spaghetti dangles from her fist. I grab a strand, place one end on my lips and slurp it toward me.

Above us we see glowing circles, overlapping to make a chain. Terese twirls a spaghetti string around her finger. It glows, too. As we speak we see the outline of our voices, or the shape of the tones, the ring of the frequencies, or, wait, we see our intestines circle above us, we see fragments up there, from our bodies. Our inner instruments have begun an unexpected band practice, ringing from the bedroom and outside the bedroom, from the plants in the backyard and in the botanical garden and from the shadow figures of the museum. Everything hums. All of Oslo's components float like a deck of tarot cards, sprinkling and flaking fragments that we can reassemble like a mandala, a whole, flaming from our own brew.

An episode:

A group of experienced witches and one apprentice hike into a field in Austre Moland on the midsummer solstice. They mow a circle of the Southern grass short using a pole made out of holly, dig a hole in the ground right in the middle of the circle and murmur a few words from a tablet with a black metallic finish.

A huge black ram appears. He has bloody horns and a wax candle strapped to his back.

The ram commands them all to greet him by kissing his behind, below the tail. The kiss immediately sends them into a trance, and they begin to dance around in circles, back to back, as the ram pisses into the hole they have dug, filling it with bright yellow urine. This is the witches' holy water.

The witches add herbs to the water, drink the holy water urine from little black goblets, and as they drink, the wax candle on the ram's mane is lit and 'Happy Birthday' begins to play.

The witches continue to dance until they pass out and slump to the ground. The ram stands quietly. Perhaps he will, in short spurts, change into a girl on all fours, dressed in black, with black hair.

'Happy Birthday' continues playing until the candle has burnt down.

The Sabbath

Let's zoom out for a moment.

The pleasant Southern cobblestone streets in the centres of Lillesand, Grimstad, Arendal, Tvedestrand and Risør lie deserted. They're easily recognised; it's not permitted to paint the listed wooden houses here any colour but white. It's completely quiet, until you gradually hear the distant sound of an engine, and then another one, and then another one; now the entire crew of furious and disruptive car cruisers are approaching. Sunday school children peek out the window of the evangelist church and see the cruisers drive back and forth, back and forth, new variations all the time. Occasionally the gang skid across a patch of lawn, a little too close to a pavement edge or a walkway. Back and forth, engines hissing as loudly as possible, squeezing out as much sound as they can.

I see them drive past, honking, from the room where I practice with my metal band in 1998. I'm standing by the window with the black microphone, in black clothes and with black hair, and for a moment I'm drawn to the cars, the drifting, rootlessness out there. The cruisers yank me out of the process I'm in, the process of creating a direction for my hatred. The music and the metal community can receive some of my hatred, and the rest has to glow undisturbed inside the music, far away from the world. But the moment the cruisers honk, we all feel, everyone in the band, that we're not far from the world after all; we're just another one of the street racers' targets. Together, we're just any other Southern congregation that can be disrupted.

Note the cruisers' routes. Draw up a map, imagine that we mark it using a running app, and see how they use their old, worn-out cars and their noisy sound systems to sketch unnecessary and impossible alternative cityscapes. The streets of these villages that they know and are trapped in become their escape routes. With black marks from skidding wheels on the asphalt, they translate and rewrite the white towns. They skip school and work to blare their horns outside the Filadelfia Pentecostal centre. At the Betania Free Evangelical centre they skid across the ice on the parking lot, until a *Parking for Visitors Only* sign tumbles to the ground. They blast Snap and Scorpions and Eminem relentlessly from the benches outside the metal venues, outside city council meetings at the town hall, and at the annual conference for the People's Movement Against Immigration. In these moments they don't discriminate, and they don't fight, they just disrupt and refuse to participate. Total misanthropy. Vodka in a Coke bottle and a cheesy ground beef sub on the dashboard. This is the Witches' Sabbath of the '90s.

In the latest ritual, Venke, Terese and I sneak past the ruins of the old Munch museum. The camera lens is zoomed all the way out now, and the image is of an undefined future, well into the next generation. We walk through the botanical garden, which looks the same as ever, with its arboretum, its alpine garden and its magical herbs. Beyond the garden is a college, the one with the classroom and the all-girls class. It's since been modernised, with screens and algorithmic surveillance systems that only we can get past.

Venke is anxious about returning to college, and stays in the rear, gnawing her cuticles.

The students are lined up in the canteen. Reconnaissance cameras identify their faces, gender, weight and height, and as they are given access to the cashier, their data, registered diets and suggestions for lunches are displayed on a screen. At the entrance, tacked above the head of a girl who whispers and laughs into a clam-shaped smart phone, a poster advertises a particularly fun salad with the caption *Seriously Excited*.

We've painted costumes on ourselves that resemble their school uniforms. Pale neon stripes blink on our dark blue jackets. Someone ahead of us in the queue turns around and looks at us in confusion – our ruffled hair, the wrinkles beneath our eyes, the big visible pores in our skin, but most of them just look into the little flowers, animals or shells that are their smart phones, or look at each other, whispering to each other and shoving. The camera looks deep into my eyes. I unfold in front of the lens, revealing all the darkness inside. The screen goes black and the *Seriously Excited* picture starts to flicker, but I'm allowed to pass. The digital noise formula that we've written seems to work. Terese winks.

At the far end of the room is a big machine with a hole in the middle where the food is delivered. The students name the dishes, and a moment later they appear on the conveyor belt, emerging from the witch's cauldron.

Oatmeal, one student says to the machine, and immediately a plastic bowl of microwaved cereal pops out.

Burger, says another one, and a thin patty in a buttered bun comes dancing out of the hole, packed in a translucent plastic box. Salad and dressing ooze and drip onto the napkin at the bottom. The food is reflected on the machine, as the small dishes flow down the little conveyor belt and are picked up by the students.

Muffin, says Terese. A compressed muffin rolls out of the machine's hole, wrapped in plastic. Everything here is portion wrapped. Nothing is served from a communal pot or bowl, only lonely meals with clear boundaries separating them from the outside world, meals made for a singular I.

Aspic, Venke says, giggling, and out comes a plate with a trembling cube of jelly on it, with peas, crab sticks and slices of hardboiled egg inside.

Don't scare them, says Terese.

Strawberry yoghurt, I say.

She should be happy I didn't say *smashed burger with béarnaise sauce*. The crown jewel of Southern junk food.

The students sit down with their food and begin to eat. We sit down with them. A girl has her head deep in a pink screen and writes a poem or a diary entry. A group of girls sit throwing salad at each other. *Seriously excited*. In the background, orders of hamburgers, cheese sandwiches and pizza slices continue to slide out from the machine. Summoned by the youths. Summoned by the words. The objects obey and emerge.

Eat slowly, says Terese to Venke, and don't play with your food. We're not supposed to stand out.

Venke picks at the aspic and starts to chew a piece, transforming fossils into new layers of fossils down in her stomach.

I open the yoghurt cup.

Normcore, Venke whispers.

The students are eating salad, hotdogs and pizza and staring at their phones. A group of girls have gotten up from their table, staring fiercely at each other. Suddenly they begin pushing each other, shouting and pulling hair.

The camera drone bobs calmly up by the ceiling, filming the scene and transmitting it directly to the teacher's lounge and the school's popular *SchoolMe* livestream.

Two girls separate from the group and begin fighting for real. They punch each other, kick, pull at each other's clothes. We realise that they are trying to grab each other's little key chains, with tiny little memory sticks hanging on them, to see what they've written about each other. Neither is willing to reveal the contents of her memory stick to the other. But sooner or later this will be unavoidable, because nothing can be deleted and the internet keeps everything in its cold cloud-storage clutch. The data already oscillates between new sponsored school-related applications. This fight won't wipe out anything. This fight can't even really be called real; it's a fight over formulas or streaming numbers. That's why there's no blood when they hit each other square on the nose or the mouth, and the spittle doesn't drip. Their clothes don't tear. Their faces won't swell.

The girls drag each other down and wrestle on the floor. There's no blood on anyone's face. The girl with the pink clamshell, who has been watching them coolly, jumps up and runs to the scene with a bottle of ketchup from the canteen counter. She begins to squirt it at the two on the floor, and the ketchup splashes over their mouths and noses and collars and arms. At one point we see a jet of blood-coloured liquid squirt across the lips of one girl as she tilts her head back.

A teacher comes to the rescue and yells something at the students that we don't hear. They glare at her but immediately stop fighting. The teacher grabs the hand of the girl with the ketchup bottle and leads her out of the room. The other combatants are left, and stand panting heavily for a moment before walking toward the classroom door, checking their phones as they go.

The rest of the students, those who sat calmly watching the scene, return to their lunch. In a moment the school bell will ring for the next class with an SMS-like ding. This usually makes the screens blink, causing the students to jerk and then rise and make their way to the classroom. But that hasn't happened yet.

While they are still sitting calmly picking at the leftovers from their portion-packaged food, the room disappears behind colours. It's as if an invisible glass wall or curtain has dropped in front of them, and this invisible curtain or wall is now being covered by splats of colour, or occult symbols, or squirts from the ketchup bottle that was just involved in the fight. Picture this: The students behind the wall move more sluggishly now, as though in slow motion, while they literally drown in colour, like crab sticks drowning in aspic. Then they are completely still, smartphones held in motionless hands, a fork frozen en route to a mouth. Frozen solid. As if the students have been rewritten into fossils, as if the wall in front of this room has stopped time, the space completely enclosed, and completely filled with something else.

The students won't notice anything; this is only a brief flash to them, during a boring school day, far beyond the colours. Without their realising it, the band in here has split their time in two, and like prawns and peas in aspic they are stuck in there, while we've opened a space between two seconds where we own the canteen, where we can remake it into our own venue.

This room between the seconds is darker. The small canteen tables have been pushed together to create a long, set dinner table. The scrape of chair legs, the buzz of chit-chat and laughter sound from corner to corner. There must be fifteen people here now. There are still more chairs than women sitting down around the table, but it's beginning to fill up. Most are older than school age, and aren't wearing a uniform. A few have been here all along, like us, disguised as students.

In the background we can hear the opening tone of the SMS-like ding that summons the students to their next class, but in the room between the seconds, time has stopped and the faint tone remains whirling in the air as food is served to us and our dinner party guests. Our food isn't portion packaged, but arrives on big platters. Everything served is soft and gelatinous, to represent the dimensions: height, width, length, time, gelatin.

More aspic, I say. That was the password for the gathering: aspic.

An enormous aspic trembles in the middle of the table; it's not as set as the one Venke ordered. In its gelatinous consistency it's reminiscent of some man-made mollusc. Around the aspic platter are other dishes with more soft, smooth food: mushy peas, jelly, boiled eggs, soft custards and cheesecakes, Norwegian lye-softened salted cod, *lutefisk*, and a pasta sauce without spaghetti, swimming in oil. The food has been decadently arranged and partly spills onto the table.

The guests, who aren't students anymore, but girls and women of all ages and shapes, start eating. We're all excited, and more concerned with talking than eating. The food jiggles on our forks in time with the conversations; after all, we are in this faintly unstable space between time zones, where stuff connects a little more loosely and everything is a little more smeared than in ordinary reality.

Where's the spaghetti? a younger girl asks. No one knows if there'll be spaghetti, or where it might be found.

Fucking hell, I say. No one reacts; everyone continues with animated conversations in different groups, but we know what's about to happen.

A new, different figure has entered the room, has perhaps already been here for a while. Someone looks up, jumps to her feet, nudging the table and making the delicate dishes jerk. The figure is dressed in black. The guests sit petrified for a moment, the food alone jiggles, nothing else moves.

The person looks like a mix of priest and demon. This new arrival stands in a corner at first, then one of the older women approaches and invites the person to sit at the table in one of the

128

empty chairs. The figure sits, politely, is served aspic on a plate but remains seated without eating. Perhaps the figure participates in the conversation.

Gradually, the guests' conversations resume. Spaghetti is requested once more. No one knows where it is this time, either.

More strangers arrive and are invited to the table. They have typical demonic characteristics, like cloaks and makeup, and some are the size of school kids, others so big they can barely sit on the chairs without crashing to the floor; they sit looking down between their legs to keep their balance. They appear masculine. One of them is completely concealed by a cloak. The demons' conversation is annoying at first; they speak slowly and their accent is archaic. But the conversation picks up when they start talking about the underworld that they're from.

One of the demons opens its cloak a little over the belly to illustrate a point and the spaghetti girl spots a spaghetti strand dangling inside. She grabs the spaghetti and starts to slurp it up toward herself. Venke claps her hands. Skin jiggles with every smack of her hands.

The girl slurps up more and more spaghetti. It turns out the body and head of this demon are made entirely of spaghetti, and it slowly begins to unravel. In the end, the cloak is the only thing left on the chair. The girl devours the last strand of pasta, and happily continues to eat what's left on her own plate. As if the demonic spaghetti isn't real food, but satisfies some other need.

The other guests start looking more closely at the new arrivals, every one of whom is now anxious and attempts to withdraw. We begin to find food scraps on the demons' bodies, and slowly devour them, every last one, in a feast that looks more and more like a brawl. The demons are made of liquorice and cocoa powder, gingersnaps and celery, artichokes, cocktail berries and pineapple rings.

I study the demon that kept its face concealed under its cloak and slowly reach my hand toward the hood, pulling it down. A face appears underneath the fabric, or an inverted face, like HR Giger's *facehugger*, that big insect larva that wraps arms and tentacles round and into the human face, covering the outside like a hand. Carefully, I sink my teeth into it. It's soft and a little viscous. I hear a faint squeal coming from inside it, and I take my first bite of a demon. It coats my mouth like a kind of gruel or almond custard. Venke and Terese and several more people stand up and approach me and together we bite, slurp and lap it all up. Under the gruel *facehugger*'s spine, a half-finished screaming face is revealed, made of hardened chocolate sauce. We eat this face too. Some dip their fingers, or a strawberry or a pineapple ring in the sauce, while I lick and suck and slurp up the face, feeling it slide down my belly like a long, warm tentacle.

Now they're all gone. That's that.

Terese is sitting on the floor under the table, where she has found one final dessert. A marzipan sausage. It's sliced and distributed around the table. We enjoy it slowly, already full and content.

One of us grabs three leftover spaghetti strands from a platter and forms a circle with each of them, like three snakes biting their own tails. Then she shifts the three rings so they partly cover each other, overlapping, like three occult Olympic rings, like the way we overlap each other, with legs, arms and chocolate sauce shared between us.

We doze lightly on our chairs and on the floor. I dip my hand in a blotch of chocolate sauce on the seat of a chair and draw shapes on the seat cover. Venke has taken out two bags and positioned herself at the end of the table. She removes red rubber gloves from one bag and puts them on, then she sticks her hand in the other. Her hand rummages through the bag. The rest of us sit up and watch. A few people start to giggle. Venke retracts the gloved hand. She's got something brown and soft in her fist. Is it even more food, custard, fondant, or is it faeces? She turns and throws the thing at the wall behind her, the one with the petrified students behind it.

Is it shit? someone yells.

Is it? Venke asks in return. Or is it mud? Is it chocolate?

The rest of us squeal with joy.

If it's shit, someone else says, then it's ours. Our waste! Human antimatter! We've got to make something with it.

Venke holds the bag up and hands out rubber gloves. Some of us put on gloves and hesitatingly start poking their hands into the shit. It might be chocolate. More squealing.

Then everyone start flinging poo around, first cautiously, then more and more wildly, at the walls and at the canvas, like a pillow fight. The mood is warm and friendly, the pitches euphoric.

The effect of the chocolate, or faeces, grows greater and more powerful, clearer, as if it's sedated us, or we've crossed some boundary. As if we're taking part in a role-play in which our real personalities are increasingly concealed, literally and metaphorically, by all the shit. Fact and fiction are snogging. We've used hallucinations for paint, and stand on the other side of the mirror, where the students could have peered over at us, were they not stuck in time. We've opened up this space and stepped over into delirium, a ritual where everything can happen. We're glued together by the faeces, like one long coiled-up snake that licks every one of its orifices, content and lazy.

A distant SMS ding is heard. Slowly the clogged room opens up again, and that one second out there in reality has become the next. It's time to leave.

Someone is pushing the painted glass walls towards each other, we get closer and closer, as the space narrows between the room in the room and the time in the time. Finally we have to head off, out, and we discover that we're no longer dirty and full, that we're no longer smeared with brown gunk. We quickly disappear from the school, in every direction, just as mysteriously as we arrived. As I exit, I hear a backward SCREECH, as if someone has lifted the needle off a spinning LP, and suddenly I'm alone. I text Venke and Terese but don't get a reply until much later, as if we've been scattered into different years on our way back to our own time and can't reach each other.

I'm not sure the ritual itself ended in erasure, as if it never happened, or if it made itself invisible by some enchantment, and is still happening now we've returned to our daily routine. It's impossible to know whether I'm covered in phantom shit or not. As a result I spend the entire day and rest of the week sniffing myself, something Venke and Terese later will confirm they did, too. None of us is sure if she smells or not, but we are all consumed by a constant hunt for clues, trying to figure out if any smell is there. We're animals that sense something, that have caught a scent, perhaps our own.

This is the magic of magic; that it's impossible to know whether it happens or not, since magic goes against reason and therefore necessarily becomes a question of faith. This afternoon in Tøyen we believe in phantom shit. It's on the outside and on the inside, in the shape of the mass we chucked at each other and the chocolate-sauce face we ate. It's magic double-sided tape, since the brown mass simmers both outside and inside us for the entire rest of the day. It burns on and under our skin, in our cheeks, in our jaws, our teeth, all around our gullet, stomach and intestines, and down toward our groins. When I close my eyes I can picture my internal form, a different form than the one I recognise as my own, a shape with new networks and escape routes marked by skidding wheels on the asphalt.

Let's rewind a little and zoom in again, on exactly that moment when the ritual ends and we're back in the ordinary chronology with the students from the canteen. Something has changed, as if systematic reality has been disrupted by the ritual. Look at all the mess in there. There's ketchup on the floor, on the walls and the ceiling, and no one seems to be wiping it up. But have a look, too, at the girls who fought, and the girl who squirted them with the ketchup bottle. The two warriors haven't left the room, and no adult has yet removed the third girl. They've just wiped their faces and hands, and now they're sitting together around a table, all three, drawing inside a square on the tabletop, laughing. The teachers are nowhere to be seen. Next to the drawing square, in the margins of the Sabbath, I write in three coke bottles and a tray of almost-finished cheesy ground-beef subs.

This is their world, but also ours. And yours too.

Total misanthropic black metal, I write within the drawing square, for the girls, or in the film document's side panel. They are all sheets in the same document, all this fabric in the same textual weave, with Venke, Terese, me and you.

I cross out *black metal* and think about the cruisers, not giving a fuck about colour, wearing distressed jeans and bleaching their hair in football patterns. They fill up their tanks with total misanthropy and its Southern twin, blasphemy. Perhaps they're still the most blasphemous of us all. They are the only ones who want to disrupt, not by setting fire to the same tame state church or singing about upside-down crosses, but by blaring the Pentecostal prayer meetings into pieces, right in the middle of the glossolalia. Through the high streets and parking lots the cruisers write, like witches, outlining another world. Misanthropy, blasphemy, cruiser magic.

Aside from the obvious reasons, I don't know why I feel I have to be able to justify my actions, or the cruisers' actions, through analysis. Maybe it's because it's important to me that what we do should mean something, that language should be able to find different strategies and be something other than a machine for shame and denial. Maybe it's because I can't let go of the idea that we have to find society's boundaries and transgress them in as many ways as possible, that we must highlight, study, analyse them, all the way down to even the most low-minded crap.

Are you also compelled to go down there?

I want to write about people and characters and places disappearing until they actually disappear, maybe becoming art, so that I'm able to believe the opposite: that art can be real. That there is a magical potential.

The Cosmic Internet

Something's out there. We become aware of it soon after the stench takes hold. It's as if the curse we cast dragged something else up with it; something that's trying to communicate with us. We sense it in the draughty windowsills, the sockets and routers in the witches' den. We have no word for it, we don't exactly know what we're talking about yet, and we end up glancing, sniffing and looking at each other without a word. We only get a whiff of it. Sometimes I feel it in the light wind created by my own fingers across the touchpad as I scroll down a website and finally ram against the bottom of the page, fingers still dragging the image down.

Venke, Terese and I take a break from gigs, rituals and film writing and start hunting in the places where we sense the whiff. We sink deep into the dark web, crypto blogs, old witch forums. We trawl through the garbage dump of the internet, through abandoned social platforms, obsolete blogs, and online news articles with formatting errors. We trawl through art archives, file registries, disks and minidisks. We play songs and videos that have never been played before. As yet we're not getting any closer to it, but searching, being on a hunt, on our way, noses to the ground, has its own value.

I consider writing *Online Witch Rituals* into the browser's Google search banner, and pressing *I'm Feeling Lucky* instead of *Search*. It's obviously a joke, and I don't do it, but I could have, and it wouldn't have mattered anyway. I realise that Google knows more about me than God.

I hate Google.

But I like scrolling. It's an easy movement, like rolling or gliding or falling, but without gravity. The action of my fingers pulls me down different websites, blogs, articles, through social media platforms. It's unstoppable, this sliding movement, and the websites seem endless. Deeper and deeper down the hole I descend from the simple search where I started, and know that if I turn around and scroll up, I will eventually come back to the beginning, but as long as I continue the descent, it'll never end.

At the start of these aimless searches, this scrolling movement seems the closest any of us can get to magic on the internet. The scrolling is a pull that emerges and exists only in movement. I feel as though, if I move my fingers fast enough, I can overtake the present and step into the future. And if the search words I type in are dark enough, I'll be able to continue down the different layers of the atmosphere and then the earth. In the end, I'll be able to scroll myself all the way to hell.

I like the idea of hell. I like how easy it is to get there. Just by thinking or writing those simple words. In 1998, when I curse loudly in front of the class, I do it because I like cursing; I've had years to cultivate the most articulate *fucking hells* and *holy shits*. The teacher knows that when I say it the words are capitalised and in a particular font, so I get a written warning. Hell is a sea of written warnings. Hell is the place God doesn't want to see, or can't see, or has ignored. When I swear I feel electric. That same year, when I use the internet connection I've set up at home, I get a similar feeling, a tingle, as if an electric signal that smoulders in my body has been amplified. I put my hand on the modem and feel the frequencies of the dial-up sound drone through me. Since then I have not been able to separate the memory of electrical shocks from loose terminal blocks and copper wiring in the broom cupboard from my memories of swearing and the descent into hell, and connecting to the internet. I just remember information streaming through the arteries in my wrists.

It takes a while for me to remember this when we first begin the search. It's been twenty years since I got internet at home, and since then the internet has changed, alongside us. Our movements and rituals across the screen are superficially similar to what we were doing twenty years ago, but the internet has long since shed its mystical skin. The haphazard searches and screen trances that we fell into in the '90s are now controlled and regulated by more mundane rituals, steady pulses between fluctuating browser banners. The movements don't lead us down to the underground, but between inbox and outbox, new page loads, post uploads, and new posts in our feed. Venke, Terese and I breathe between applications, we slip in and out of images, as if the internet were no longer a mystical dimension but a rhythmic imitation of life. Above us the algorithms watch over our actions, on earth as in heaven.

But then we really get going, and although we're distracted, prevented and interrupted, we find the undertow is still there. We can still feel the hatred surge through our veins. We've found a direction for our search now, but what follows we don't know. We've stopped switching banners and applications in time with our breath. It's as if we're rediscovering the internet and wandering through the ruins of the museum of interrupted connections, outside the all-consuming portals. We've yet to find anything else, but we do feel an ever-growing presence. Maybe what we're supposed to find isn't a particular place, but a process, a recipe, a code, a combination of keyboard shortcuts, a language. We begin to feel that old sensation of electricity surging from the power grid and into our bodies. Late at night, long after darkness has fallen both outside and inside the apartment because we forgot to turn on the light, we lift our gazes from our computers and see each other's eyes glow like predators'.

Inside the witches' den, we scan and scroll our way down, with fingers and noses and eyes and external hard drives. The internet isn't deep enough. Sooner or later it'll stop and something else will take over. Hatred glows in the palms of hands hovering above keyboards. That's how writing begins, I think, not with a document or a text or a word, but with this glow, this prickling.

Dear internet,

The electricity in my hands is palpable now, and I'm starting to remember just how much machines meant to me, how high my hopes for the internet once were. I remember playing pretend-internet on computers as far back as 1989, before I knew it existed.

This internet-before-the-internet game is my first ritual project. I draw the same things over and over again in the application Paint, as if I were waiting for someone else to continue the drawing for me, or with me. I talk to the hard drive when I play games and open programs in MS-DOS.

It's the same year I get really into *Superman 3*. I watch the film every weekend. I'm especially obsessed with the ending, where the oblivious bad guy Gus Gorman – played by a tremulous Richard Pryor, uncharacteristically free from profanity – has constructed a giant computer that suddenly breaks free from human control. In the process it attracts several of the main villains into its machine body. It then wraps cords and machinery around the villains, making them hybrid creatures; organic robots in the service of the computer. The villains receive wireless information from the horrific machine through invisible waves through space, or somehow at least they know what to do to hunt Superman and the other good characters. They have cords and metal plates on their faces, but still resemble themselves. As robots they are half living and half dead; they speak the words of the machine with their own voices, like mediums, or like Pentecostals speaking in tongues.

In the middle of my *Superman* obsession I go to the hospital to visit grandma, who is recuperating after a surgery; various wires and hypodermic needles are connected to her body, saline solution, medication, something that looks like blood. All the wires make me dizzy, and I think about the machine people from *Superman 3*. Before then, I've never really thought about the body as real and mortal; that we also have to be plugged into something and get support to live sometimes.

Does it hurt? Can you feel anything? I ask grandma, as I poke at one of the wires.

I feel for that lady over there, she replies and gestures across the room at a woman in a coma, surrounded by just as many wires and drip stands.

The comment is inscrutable to me, but when I think about it several years later I realise it's true: they are both plugged into the containers and walls of the hospital. Their body tissue communicates with the wires, with the fluids and the plastic and the metal, perhaps also with each other's tissue, and even with me as I drink red Ribena from a plastic cup and eat liquorice from the vending machine in the hallway.

As I continue to draw increasingly macabre illustrations in Paint, writing love letters to computers and mocking God with demonic quartertones in the school choir, the modern internet really starts taking shape around the world. Different versions of Russian and French networks have already existed, but this year, while grandma and the other woman at the hospital are plugged into the machines and the walls and each other, various successors to ARPANET (Advanced Research Projects Administration) are connected to each other, too, and this larger network is called the internet. The connections are material, but the web is perceived as something else: it's understood as a virtual dimension where we could potentially contact anyone at any time. Without my realising it, we are connected to a global heart-lung machine, that a few years later will promise to pump our virtual blood between us, unrestricted and uncensored.

The internet was kind of spiritual in the '90s, wasn't it? Terese says.

I was looking for someone to talk to, I say.

Me, too, says Venke, the dial-up was like a ringtone. Like ringing God.

The Jesus teens don't talk about the internet in that way in the '90s. Maybe they feel that same electric surge through their hands when they fold them in prayer. And maybe I'm looking for something on the network, too, when a few years later I begin to surf the internet and chat on mIRC, first one night per week in a classroom and later at home. It always disappoints me that the ones I'm chatting to are real people from Ås, or San Diego or Johannesburg. Between the chat shifts, I dream up better conversations than the ones that exist in the real logs, and I continue to write to the computer, to invisible partners deeper in the

143

mechanical systems. The feeling in my fingers as they rest on the warm keyboard reminds me of spiritualism. It's the closest I get to communing with the spiritual realm. The electricity, the network, the connection. The internet is all I need to connect to another world, to disappear into another world, get away, or just feel close to something mystical and impossible. I fantasise about finding my own doppelgänger on the internet, or that I will suddenly be chatting to a version of myself from the future, or chatting to my grandma through the machines. A few years later I will be googling myself to sleep at night in imaginary search engines.

In the witches' den, with Terese and Venke, I type into the search bar *the internet as a spiritual force*. I delete it and instead type *How the spiritual world is like the internet*. I delete this too and write *Find God on the internet*. I don't press Search, but I am searching.

Dear God, who art online.

In my witch's den in Oslo in the early 2000s I study for my bachelor's degree; I've long since become a nerd, like Gus Gorman in *Superman 3*, only a little more destructive. Of all the students taking the mandatory IT course, I get along best with the program. Not technically – I can't even make the Word document black – but I'm the one devoting the most time to what I hope is the magic of the machine. I'm the one who fantasises about being an HTML code and being held in the arms of the brackets. I'm the one forever inventing clever and cleverer Alta Vista searches, as if I were flirting with the browser. I'm the quickest at finding smut and illegal MP3s. The rest learn good work methods and routines. I work my way into and down the internet and find *Deep Throat* and *Sweet Movie*. Even when I communicate with other people, via Messenger or email or mIRC, I'm mostly concerned with the computer screen and the programs, and later the laptop and the smartphone and the applications. I'm always communicating with them too. I study keyboards and the sound of buttons, I breathe in the electricity, and the eternal scrolling movement makes me zone out long before the internet achieves that seemingly endless stream.

Then the internet grows, and it quickly changes from something deep, mystical and soft, like body tissue, into big, lumpy, stultifying portals and programs. In the computer courses and later in the programming classes, there's no longer room to search for connection or community through the web and the programs. It's not about the web at all; the web is invisible, something that just has to work, and the programs are just tools, codes you have to master. I resist for a while, continue to search the deep and find stuff no one else finds, or write clunky, unnecessary Java arguments to make the program short-circuit. For a while I approach the internet the way I do religion and the South, as a wall I have to break down and a system I have to destroy. And then, I become what we call grown-up, and the internet becomes what we call grown-up, and we abandon each other, automate our interactions, surrender to muscle memory and necessity.

Look me deep in the algorithms. It's as if the internet's entire underground potential has vanished into their archives. The pull the internet has on me lies dormant, reduced to something unconscious and functional, memorised grips on metal frames and finger constellations on the phone case. I shape my body gently around the machines, hand resting like a soft pillow under my phone as I text. Even now, as I write this to you, my upper body hangs over the laptop like a cradling breast, or am I the one that's held by it? Maybe we're both suckling each other at the same time. All this time I've participated in a ritual where I extend myself into the machine, without thinking about it as an extension of me.

Through the evening darkness in our witches' den, I see Venke and Terese behaving in the same way with their tablets and laptops in the kitchen, and together we watch the neighbours participate in the same patterns. They walk cautiously around their apartments, rocking their applications as if they were rocking children to sleep. This is probably how I've always wanted to be rocked and comforted, by the metaphysical place with the biggest arms, the arms of the internet.

Routine machine rituals aren't magical, I say, still in the kitchen.

But they could have been, says Terese. They have potential. Imagine everything we remember now, everything we've forgotten.

Venke is deeply absorbed in an old sewing kit next to her laptop. She's gotten excited by the image of a machine and man nursing each other. She sits cutting little bits of sewing thread from the kit and tying the threads around her nipples, where they press against her jumper.

Isn't that image just a metaphor for the echo chamber? I say. Life in the self-referential circuit, and the dependency that keeps us there. When did we get to this place?

Even the echo chamber has potential, Venke argues.

Her nipples are now poking out beneath her jumper, and she ties them together with a new piece of thread. Now they are connected like an infinity loop.

They're the same figure, says Terese, the echo loop. The little, anxious subject suckling its own body, all alone.

But the loop doesn't exist in a vacuum, says Venke: imagine it as a movement, a feeling, a connection.

She raises a pair of scissors to cut the end of the thread that's still attached to the spool, but instead cuts the loop right between her nipples. The threads fall away from each other, only to grow toward each other again. Down on the table the spool jerks. The threads around each nipple reconnect in new forms and loops from the thread under Venke's upper body, and it starts to move, forming new bonds, weaving a steadily growing network of loops and figures around itself.

Our father, who art in hell, I say, and we all laugh.

The nipples poking out of Venke's jumper are no longer just nipples, but also buttons, doorknobs, corks or the heads of plastic screws. Like characters on a keyboard, they can be pressed, held and combined, creating various syntheses. The strings twist them in different directions, and suddenly we hear this growing, piercing metallic sound, like what you hear on the underground before trains arrive in the station. Two thin metal threads then emerge, pushing their way out from each tip and flowing down her upper body like a set of glistening train tracks. Just as we understand what's going on, they disappear again. The magical moment is over. But maybe the threads are still there, stretching around us, around me and Terese too, as if from Gus Gorman's uncontrollable machine, the one that folded its thin copper wires around our faces. The atmosphere in the room is still electric. This is the extension, this tingle, and the glow we're looking for.

This moment is the first we've seen of a different set of connections. We keep looking, in all the forgotten Wi-Fi connections, the ones that don't make sense. In all the connections that don't involve a lonely subject under God's gaze. If we can hex Oslo, we can dig up whatever it is we're looking for from the internet too.

What began as a mere sensation is beginning to take form, the form of another internet. We're starting to hear the drone more clearly now, inside echoing sound effects and programs with compilation errors, far down the deep web. And we hear it from other places too. It calls to us when we water the tomato plants near the modem. We've started to notice little formations and signs in the steam from the teakettle, not so different from the threads growing around Venke's jumper, as if all around us new life forms are emerging. We notice that when we see these signs, the ordinary internet becomes difficult to use. The router blinks yellow, is interrupted or made useless by a hellish mess. Spam flows unfiltered into the inbox and videos we didn't search for start playing on the screen, like a poltergeist throwing things around inside our machines.

Terese, Venke and I christen this internet *the cosmic internet.*

Dear god, you can't touch this, says Terese.

And then we switch the internet off. We imagine that the search will be easier without it. Instead, we daisy-chain our computers and create a communal text document, a hex dialogue between them. This time we're going to track down the cosmic internet ourselves. We'll summon it side by side, at the kitchen table in the witches' den.

The cosmic internet communicates through noise, we note in our dialogue. It creates confusion, poor connections, pixelated images and digital one-way streets. If it's discovered, it'll be banned immediately, but since the government will never be completely sure it exists, within the existing definitions of existence, the legislation will have to be abstract and ineffective, incorporated with grey writing in the documents' annoying and disruptive grey areas, meaning margins, notes and footnotes. It will remain unexplored bonus material.

The cosmic internet can hardly be used for money transfers, shopping, credit checks or advertising, Venke writes.

But it will be possible to transmit cosmic internet signals through the bank's fibre optics, making money straight up disappear from their numeric systems, I argue.

Or maybe transform the numbers to a stinking mass of fat, oozing from the USB ports, Terese suggests, inspired by her sourdoughs.

USB-pores, I reply.

The cosmic internet is an ancient witch commune, don't you think? Venke writes.

Sounds a little esoteric, I type back. Couldn't it be for everyone?

It's an open network, Venke replies immediately.

It can be fuelled by human matter, and the electricity from our own bodies, Terese replies, and I add that that's at least how my hands feel right now.

We agree that in the long run, when it trusts us, the web will evolve into a fleshy peer-to-peer network, where a small part of your flesh is always seeding.

It won't hurt, but you'll feel it in the form of connections and sensations occurring in the body.

Collective phantom limbs, Venke fantasises; anatomical phantom eyes, Terese suggests; portals, I hammer on, where THE SPACE BAR ejects us into space. The temperature rises in the witches' den.

It shouldn't distinguish between body and data, or living and dead, Venke writes, and presses the point even though she can hear Terese giggling next to her.

We agree that in the most extreme instances, you should be able to log on to the cosmic internet and exchange small pieces of flesh with other bodies out there in the hereafter, and then feel a leg or an arm snatched at, as your body comes into contact with the half-composted dimensions.

A carnal version of how we first perceived the internet? I write.

It could be a carnal version holding the possibility of contact with the hereafter, the spiritual. Like that time when electricity felt so new that it gave us the sensation of extension into new dimensions, proof that there's something out there. The cosmic net could be a place where you actually get there. Where you type into the search bar *Is anybody out there?* And then press ENTER and SPACE.

That's where we can meet. That's where we can write. That's how I want to write. Now, I'm writing.

We're writing. As we write, the click of the keys sounds more and more like the cracking of little bones. As we finish for the night, we joke about how we can see constellations of stars and bits of skeletons glittering in the black screens that sleep in front of us: little dots from the universe, and pieces of ourselves. Later, back at mine, I can feel the jerk of a leg, or is it an arm, the way my body jerks when I dream I'm falling. At the same time I hear a noise, like the short echo of an old modem that is dialling and connecting. It's the call of the cosmic internet, or the dial-up. Maybe I'm logged on when I sleep, when I let myself scroll down my consciousness, let go of my waking existence. When I'm free to search for you. ENTER, SPACE.

It's day again. Our witch's cauldron, a private Google doc we share, is seething and boiling with ingredients found in deep places. It's a red herring, deployed to distract the ordinary internet from our actual task.

Somewhere else, on other screens, far from the reach of the algorithms, magical image searches are scrolling hurriedly past, with their tidy rows of tiny little preview pictures:

One of us, wearing a mask that obscures her face, holds the sun in her hand.

Another, painted like a Munch figure with eyes like deep dark holes, grips a paint brush in her hand.

Someone, face painted like a panda with deep dark holes for eyes, grips her pubic hair in her hand. Glitter, or glittering dandruff, drizzles to the ground.

Two paint brushes dripping with black and red paint are held one over the other and taped together to make a cross, perhaps an upside-down cross.

One of us holds the other's hair in their hand.

The one who is painted like a Munch figure chews on her hair.

We cut each other's hair. Blond and brown hairs, as fine as dog fur, fill a bathtub to the brim.

Imagine. This is our ritual, my ritual, your ritual. Imagine us as layers and layers of fabric and textures, layers and layers inside my film, portals to other places, Venke inside Terese inside me and all deeper inside the deepest web, where the electricity prickles.

The scrolling continues, and now the pictures form an unbroken shooting script.

A hand holds up a little pixelated chick, transferred via Skype on a terrible mobile network, giving it a blurry beak and only half a left wing. The chick shakes a few water droplets off its fur and then it settles in the hand, silent as a cutlet. Then we let it slide from hand to hand, from mouth to mouth, from armpit to armpit, between us. The chick is cradled in our bodies.

Imagine that this is a music video but that the only movement in the picture is vertical scrolling. Your own index and middle finger dragging themselves down the screen.

We gently lay the chick down in the bathtub. It rolls up into a little yellow ball of down in all our blond, brown, and grey hair and immediately falls asleep. The down pixels glitter like diamonds. We place the paint brush cross in the middle of the tub, like a mast with flaming sails, and send the tub out to sea, from the seawater pool, toward Hoved Island (ENTER, SPACE). The hair burns and the chick burns. But it's a magical chick, and it's been brought to life by the words and the image and it's not the same as a chick from reality.

This chick didn't come from an egg, but from Skype. For all we know, this chick is flame resistant.

For all we know, this floating bathtub exists, on its way out of the Oslo fjord. For all we know, it's the real chicks, and the real internet and the real rituals and the real fjord and the Barcode buildings deep in the fjord's armpit and the real black metal bands, that aren't here.

The Magic

In 1989, I love connect-the-dots. I'm really too old for them, and should be doing my own drawings from scratch, but I only do that on the computer, where everything becomes abstract and weird. If I draw on paper, the pictures just turn into horses, or boring humans and houses. I like that the lines between the dots make little cartoon characters, plants or animals appear on the sheet. I'm drawing them, but I could have never drawn them without the dots. It reminds me of how I will later imagine the internet. I'm just a hand. Like the hand that summons the words of the dead on a Ouija board.

Have you ever thought about how the Norwegian word for hand, HÅND, contains the whole word for spirit, ÅND?

Connect-the-dots drawings mimic the act of establishing contact with the spirits. We're dots, and the lines around us complete the connections between us and all others, humans and Gods, spirits, the magical beings and the underground creatures and the otherworldly beings. Before we connect the dots with lines, it's impossible to see what shape anything has.

Consider how in Norwegian the word bond, BÅND, contains the entire word for spirit, ÅND.

Let's leave this community in the witches' den once again and rewind a little, back to the time before I meet Venke and Terese, the time when I still work alone and do what I call *art*. On a tour, my stage makeup streaks in the summer heat and someone in the audience throws a roll of toilet paper on stage. I start to wipe my face, and then I wind a little of the paper around myself and continue doing other things, the roll still on the stage edge. An audience member grabs the roll and wraps TP around herself, too, before passing the roll to the person next to her. For a while the roll simply passes from hand to hand, but then more audience members start twisting a bit around themselves before sending the roll on to new hands. Finally we're connected, all of us, in an abstract starry constellation, on and in front of the stage in that grubby gallery in Richmond, Virginia.

The act makes me happy. I realise that what the audience is doing with the loo paper makes me happier than the art I'm trying to create onstage. Maybe that's how they feel, too. There are so many dots in the world, and so few of them get lines drawn between them, so few drawings are given a shape. Far too few bodies are connected. We think we see the world and its shapes in what we call reality, but we actually just see the dots that are chosen for us, the same identities that a CCTV-camera sees, lonely identities, identified and alone in the universe.

CV Dazzle is a particular kind of makeup that's used to confuse TV cameras. It can take the shape of series of dots on the face, without lines between them, or of lines in illogical places, preferably made up in colours that reflect light, to prevent cameras recognising you. It's a connect-the-dots drawing in reverse, removing the connections in a face. Human faces are reduced to dots for the camera and perhaps only then can they remain human for themselves. No camera algorithm has the settings to register the loo-roll drawing. The audience creates a collective CV Dazzle, a network constructed of the cheapest and most primitive material, a roll of toilet paper.

The experience does something to me: it's as if the loo roll has created a new organism, a new life that I never thought *art* could create. Maybe that's why I cancel the tour, leave Virginia and travel into the wilderness. Aimlessly, I drive through Tennessee, Arkansas and Texas and finally end up somewhere south of New Mexico. The desert air up here in the highlands is thinner and clearer, the sky wider, the ground, the earth less significant. New Mexico is 80 per cent sky and 20 per cent scorched red mountains, cacti and tufts of grass. My feet only barely hold on to the ground, my fingers barely reach down to the keyboard. No wonder the people around me wear thick boots and stiff, heavy hats. They've got to keep themselves grounded.

I'm so limited here. My eyes aren't enough, or my feet, or my lungs. I can't take it in. The sunset is bloody. The earth is red. If I empty my water bottle by the roadside, it dyes the sand blood-red. The laptop is full of radioactive red sand. The buttons spark.

The sounds of barking dogs, lightning strikes, and chirping birds are heard more precisely through the clear air, projecting unobstructed from beaks, snouts, and clouds straight into my ears. The sound sends impossible line drawings to Mexico, a stone's throw away, and back again. The clear air constructs layers of ancient borderlines and crossings. From the roadside overlooks I can see the curve of the earth. The horizon is the longest line of writing.

The mountains, the clouds, the sound, the borders, everything feels more soluble. I'm closer to the sky, this immense space, and at the same time, at 1,350 metres above sea level my own spaces, the smallest spaces, blood vessels and nerves and cells, are expanded. Everyone has to breathe more heavily here; the air molecules are bigger. When I breathe more deeply, I think about the world BREATHE, and how close it is to WRAITH, because with that extra force, I inhale something unknown, something extra, perhaps some local Jumano spirits. Outer space includes the sky too, I think: it begins all the way down on the ground.

I wish I'd thought that sentence in Norwegian, but the most common Norwegian word is VERDENSROMMET, meaning *world's space*, implying that space itself is part of our world, which doesn't sound right. I could of course just translate *outer space* directly; *outer*'s a Norwegian word, too, but the phrase isn't in everyday use and I don't remember it until later. Perhaps intentionally; perhaps I'm trying to get away from my own language. OUTER SPACE couldn't substitute for WORLD'S SPACE anyway, a word that doesn't exist in English. In English everything is outside of the earth, and the atmosphere is a separate space. The English language looks past the world as we know it, while the Norwegian language is actually capable of calling outer space WORLD SPACE, forcing the unknown into itself, into its silent letters, into the white. Here in New Mexico, using the Norwegian word feels ridiculous. The sky is too alien, and Mexico is too far away, fenced off behind a tall wall. Both are outer space.

A small sandstone building in the middle of no man's land is flanked by telescopes and plaques that hint at UFO sightings. In front of the building is a dark blue minibus full of metal scraps and fabric that seems to be parked there more or less permanently. An old striped cat rests in the car's shadow.

Voices sound through the clear air. A group of girls stand behind the building, looking at the sky through the telescopes. They're excited, pointing and discussing. Far up there, you can make out a tiny white dot. It moves steadily closer and the girls try to zoom in on it with the telescopes, but like most things that are free and public here in America, the lenses are low-quality, too weak to really magnify anything. Several cars begin to park and people step out to look at the dot.

The Norwegian South has its own history of white dots in the sky, retold as 'The wonderful heavenly vision above Grimstad centre 15 June 1934.' From out of a blurred white spot, far out above the fjord, a figure of Christ appeared between two puffs of clouds, first with its arms raised to the sky and then with them stretched out gently, palms facing heaven. According to witnesses he looked like Bertel Thorvaldsen's famous sculpture, as if even Christ understood that it's art and not religion that expands human space, the place that opens up imagination and faith.

In the desert by the sandstone buildings, the group of girls and a few families in cowboy hats and I stand in a circle waiting for the white to appear. We're a band now. We look in the same direction; we talk about other celestial bodies we've seen, about what we think it might be. We hold on to the same fence and pass around the binoculars. It turns out to be a border patrol drone, a modern UFO (or Christ), one of the scouts of the establishment in search of modern aliens, a plastic bone in the bone-white

American police state's skeleton, with its little helicopter arms raised from its body and up toward the sky. For a while it circles us, scanning us, then it gradually shrinks into the sky again, as if it, too, is slowly devoured, slowly loses function until it's a completely ordinary balloon, rising and rising into the atmosphere's thinner and thinner air. Finally it just blinks in and out of sight, like a mirage, or the reflection of a moving lens. Around it, clear skies in every direction, if only eyes could take them all in, or if only there were other ways to float up there, deeper and deeper into the cerulean body.

From El Paso in southern Texas I drove along the border fence, then north across the state line and into New Mexico, to a town called Las Cruces. After the drone surveillance incident, I move on to Alamogordo, an old military barracks town, and finally to insignificant little Carizzozo with its empty streets and burnt-out gas stations. Carizzozo is right next to Carizzozo Malpaís, a dark belt left by a lava stream from the volcano Little Black Peak, 5,000 years ago. The earth in this belt is completely blackened and barren; it's like walking across the remains of a burnt-out witch's bonfire. The local camping site is called Valley of Fires Recreation Area and is on a small island of rusty desert dirt surrounded by black. Most of the buildings are closed for renovation, and when I turn on the camp's standpipe I hear only the sound of a faint wind in there, like the drain into a tomb.

Not far from the malpaís is more burnt dirt of an entirely different kind: Trinity Site, scene of the first atom bomb test explosion, 16 July 1945, postponed for three days because of bad weather. The Trinity bomb was based on the fission process: atoms, once regarded as indivisible, exploded or were torn apart. Trinity's power came from splitting atoms in two. It rose through the atmosphere, a glowing, mushroom-shaped erection fantasy, with the aid of Oppenheimer's technology, the United States' immense defence budget and the modern establishment's unwavering faith in the logical binary division of the universe.

The biblical creation process is a story about fission, too, or at least a version of it. The first man, Adam, originally contained both masculine and feminine forces, united by the inevitable seam of cosmic threads. Adam was in this way completely androgynous, but then, according to the myth, they were unhappy with their own bisexuality, and as preparation for the universe, they cast out their feminine parts to become purely masculine. Only then could divine power shine from his eyes – from those reformed, straight eyes.

For scientists and philosophers, the atom bomb had the potential to become something more than a total meltdown of atoms and a catastrophe for mankind. Trinity and its successors could be conclusive evidence of a divine power, impelled by the pure masculine symbolism of a process that split its own components, casting off the waste to create the most powerful force of energy humanity had ever seen. Perhaps that's why the research programme behind Trinity, Little Boy and Fat Man was named the Manhattan project. Casting off the feminine parts made it possible to rise, surging with inhumane power up toward the sky, like a skyscraper, with an architecture that united Christianity, capitalism and patriarchy in a holy trinity, horny for God.

I identify with the feminine parts, those left scattered around Adam's body, the trash left behind by mankind's fusion with God. The atomic waste is invisible; it has long since been dumped and buried underground, beneath towns and neighbourhoods populated by minorities and poor people. But out here in the desert, another kind of masculine waste glitters in the dry sunlight. The area is populated by oil field and military workers, and they've scattered their empty beer cans, used condoms, junk food containers and petrol cans across the landscape. It's a modern version of the ram heads in Georgia O'Keeffe's paintings. In front of her never-ending New Mexico landscape, she displays the universe's sacred waste: the skeletons float in the air, in front of mountains, sand and sky. They glisten; they are made of the salt of the earth and the sugar of witchcraft.

What a disappointment it must have been for God's scientific apprentices when they discovered the even more powerful fusion technology. In 1952 Operation Ivy detonated the fusion bomb Ivy Mike, equivalent to ten megatons of TNT, and even at that point the men of the establishment had begun to pull out of the American nuclear project. These bombs are a dead end, they thought; the potential destruction is too great. They hadn't said that about Little Boy or Fat Man. But the fusion bomb really could blow the world as we know it to pieces. This process fuses atoms instead of splitting them; it brings isolated parts together into new forms that previously couldn't exist. I imagine the fusion bomb as a recording of Adam's gender-splitting process, the whole of genesis, in reverse, a restoring of the masculine and feminine into one condition, an impossible dimension, a *join-the-dots* feast.

A perfect blasphemous construction built in the name of piety. Ivy is both a boy's and a girl's name. Has someone made a superhero figure of Ivy?

Here in the malpaís, the scorched sand belt right next to Trinity's melted circle, I feel the presence of the atoms as they always are, inside us, always moving. They own us, contain us and disintegrate us. When I rub my hands together, the atoms are closer to each other; perhaps a few even fuse between my wrists, heated by the desert sun. What I'm feeling is the atoms' potential. I'm standing on the black belt, wondering if there were witches among the atom researchers in the '40s and '50s. Because if you learned to fuse atoms, you would also be able to see that the melting process doesn't just unify two parts; there's also a third, meddling component, an unnecessary addition, dust in the plug, a part that contributes to chaos, the original chaos. Atom, atom, *and?* Masculine, feminine, *and?*

When the hydrogen bomb Tsar Bomba was detonated in 1961, the whole world's elite trembled, not just because it was the most destructive weapon ever created, but because a bigger potential for *and?* had never been observed. The potential and the transgression found in the atoms could be transferred to philosophy, music, literature, film. That very same year, Věra Chytilová directed her first film, Agnès Varda made *Cléo from 5 to 7*, and Meredith Monk had her first solo performance. Shortly after, Roland Barthes began to write *The Death of the Author*, Luce Irigaray finished her master's degree in psychology, and Jacques Derrida began to jot down ideas for the lecture he would give at John Hopkins University in 1966.

After stopping in the Valley of Fires, I travel as close to the Trinity Site as I can get. There are no official signs or buildings in the area, just the odd roadside bench, boarded-off gravel roads and a single cardboard placard with something or other about the crater on it, probably hung there by an individual conspiracy theorist. The road into the crater is closed permanently, like most country roads in America that aren't freeways or highways. When the map application shows me I'm nearby, I stop to look around at a garish rest stop, but all I can see is reddish brown desert hills, bone-dry shrubs and a run-over UFO badge on the ground. The next day, at the National Museum of Nuclear Science in Albuquerque, I see bits of the glass that the desert sand was melted into during the bomb detonation. The matter is called trinitite, green like kryptonite, inside a dusty display case. A Geiger counter is exhibited above it as a demonstration. It crackles as it registers the atom's processes. The sound of radio-activity. Trinitite is still too fresh to touch, too pure and masculine. Or is it we who are too frail, and allow ourselves to be radiated, are we too feminine, *and?*

Here, right here, in front of the display case with trinitite, the film starts. Here I can write.

In 1997, too old now for connect-the-dots, I'm stretched out in the witches' dorm after practice with the metal band, watching German late-night television in secret. Every weekend they show soft-core porn films. I've been watching them for years already. I know the narrative style, the scenarios, the boundaries, the humour. My favourite scenes in these films are the ones where people are having sex but then can't pull apart, the so-called *penis captivus*, when the vagina's muscles are clamped around the penis with such power that it's stuck. *Penis captivus* is as good as nonexistent in reality, but a frequent feature in the world of soft-core porn. One such scene: a group of nuns encounter a couple who are making love. The ensuing panic causes *penis captivus*.

Soft-core porn presents these scenes as comical, but the humour is founded on the relationship between sex and sin. Porn's existence is founded on sin. It's no accident that a group of nuns is the catalyst for the penis's plight. The soft-core world presents as a Catholic confession, duly followed by penance. Young novices enjoying themselves with candles after bedtime, church servants and priests coveted by old mother superiors, and the men of the church wreaking havoc on young girls in their congregation and in the convent. There's an entire subgenre called *nunsploitation*. It's easy to comprehend and easy to construct a plot about how sex is illegal and suppressed and therefore particularly exiting and blasphemous. As a result, conditions like *penis captivus* occur, as if God himself intervened and punished the naughty application of genitalia. Sex consistently results in unwanted, humorous and degrading consequences.

But in these scenes of *penis captivus*, there's something else afoot, something beyond guilt: a fusion of the atoms between penis and vagina, a Tsar Bomba, or perhaps something more: an addition, a creative line, a join-the-dots, a usually invisible and impossible bond between people, perhaps Siamese, perhaps radioactive and perhaps magical. Subtitles emerge for me, when I watch soft-core porn, a map of the infinite possible relations between an infinite number of people.

Contemporary hard-core porn is different: Puritan, American, evangelical. It reflects Protestantism. Following the golden era of the '70s, hard-core porn becomes increasingly commercialised, smooth and tight. The oversized penises are only displayed erect. It's efficient and low-budget, with clean canvases; the plotting is minimal and offers fewer consequences. The guilt isn't in the desire or in the story; it's transferred to the object, presented in the form of close-ups of female genitalia and other orifices. It gives the impression of being a documentary, with every scene concluding in a *money shot* where the penis pulls out of the hole so that I, the audience, can see the cum and confirm that the plot is real. There are no muscles in any orifices, no fuckability, holding it back. The penis is not *in captivus*, it's independent and strong, like a mushroom cloud or a skyscraper rising toward the horizon. At the same time, it's cleansed of bonds, connections, viruses and magic.

Outside the school library, the girls from Jesus Revolution are discussing the moment when something becomes sex. I'm seated behind the glass wall reading, but end up listening. The girls try to define exactly where the boundary is; exactly when to stop. When does God come into the picture, when does God cum, when does something become sex? Is it the moment your boyfriend's tongue slips in between your lips and you're making out? I can't hear too much through the glass wall, but I think they conclude that the tongue isn't allowed because it's a physical metaphor for penetration. Other girls talk less; for them, metaphors don't count, and sixteen-year-olds have oral and anal sex (magical sex), because it's not sex as long as it doesn't touch the sacred hymen, the proof of innocence, the righteousness of woman, the veil that God's eye sees right through, the connection between heaven and hell.

The hard-core porn aesthetic resembles the imagery in the evangelical worldview. Desire, taboo and guilt (the holy *Trinity*) are all incorporated into the fetish objects. No one desires another person in hard-core porn: only objects are desirable. The person fucking, usually a man, is just an innocent victim of something sinful and fuckable. It can be reduced to a protestant maths equation: desire equals guilt, and it has to be distributed at the bottom of the hierarchical chain. The guilt is pushed down on the object, the body that's being penetrated. The resulting hard-core porn is the proof of the equation. The protestant equation is in this way so relentless that it becomes pornographic itself. True protestant love.

Think about it: in my language, the word LOVE, *kjærlighet*, contains the entire word TRUST, *ærlighet*. Norwegian love is 80 per cent honesty, 80 per cent confession, bowing your head to the powers of definition, naked in the face of God, truth and honesty, love and honour, the money shot. Is love, in Norwegian, hard-core? Is it cleansed of bonds and magic?

But even the hard core contains a residue, 20 per cent mysticism and hope of transgression. If we forget submission and fetish and sin, there's always something else. If you look closely enough, there's always a clit in the throat, or a strange way of chewing gum, or a camera reflected in an eye, or an eye that looks like an egg. Even for the Jesus girls there's always a handkerchief gone astray, a bare neck under the ponytail, a glass window flashing a rainbow into their mouths or along their zippers. There's always an escape route from structure and rhetoric.

There has to be room for them, too, these escape routes. I don't just write to analyse; analysis can so easily become judgemental, categorical and clean-cut. Judgement only sends our actions underground, where they can continue to play out. But in analysis we lose ourselves and our desire, we lose the escape routes and the hatred. I want to enter the hard-core image now, enter and transgress, change the plot, put the penis in *captivus*, paint the screen black, watch the film backward. Maybe if I watch it enough times I'll find something, like with the poo ritual in *Sweet Movie*. Maybe if I splice them together in writing, or into other films, into a shooting script or a film script that doesn't belong to any film, if I splice together the cum shots into a white river that's nauseating to watch, I'll find something. I can fuse, I can be Operation Ivy, superhero Ivy, I can be a virus. I can infect porn with complex desire. The desire to find something, to dig out new meanings. The desire for hatred.

The virus is the standard metaphor for the diseased elements of society, which sometimes spread quickly and dangerously, and sometimes cause a slow disintegration, rotting social democracies and nation states. Black metal has been called a virus, and homosexuality and porn culture and the Southern cruisers. The disease the virus causes spreads through the body and constructs a pattern for a new shape. It's a communal, painful language that can infect us all. Influences connect people, bring us down and together, equalise us. Virus is a bond, after all.

I dig VIRUS out of the word LOVE. I dig it out of I. I'm still looking for a bond. Or is that just something I etch into my memory to get closer to you, to make you a little more me? I'm looking for someone who can bring me closer to something. Dots I can line myself up between. Is that what I'm looking for in you? We share the same virus, I carry it for you, from you, on. *Virus captivus.*

Let's turn over the layers of pages, scenes, fabric, texture, character and images from porn, till we come to the iconic Japanese woodblock print *Octopi and pearl diver* from 1814. In this image, a woman lies on her back by a beach while two octopi pleasure her. One octopus has its head between her legs; the other is by her side caressing her chest and her mouth. Magic, fantasy, ecstasy.

Genitals are already sea creatures. Wet and soft, from birth till death. We can only ever partly understand and grasp this. Like the sound of our voices and the blood that streams from our body, they are human osmosis, just as much connected to the world as to us. They represent something infinite and only partly real to our realist eyes. They are sluggish semi-fungi, partly submerged in water, moist, smooth, slick, perforated, born eyeless. They are half human matter and half imaginary creature. That's why we have a separate sensory register for tentacles, molluscs and shellfish. The first time I try to eat octopus I have such a strong reaction I think I'm allergic: I get hot, sweaty, red, salty, foggy. But maybe what I'm actually feeling is sensory empathy, a cannibal cautiousness.

The sex is my internal organ, on the outside. My amphibian part. Genitalia displace my existence, distort the bond between life and death, matter and metaphor, land and sea. I extend myself physically out of myself. Fact and fiction meet and rub against each other, fill me up, smudge me, caress me.

I've seen a picture of my own intestines, taken during a gastroscopy while I was at university. It's a world where all sci-fi dreams meet, directly beneath my own ribs. The doctor shows me the image while I'm still woozy from the general anaesthetic, and I can remember seeing a foggy, strange planet, a soft landscape that coils in toward a narrow iris. I look deeper and deeper into my own spiralling muscle. The doctor gestures and tells me I have an illness that has worn down my intestinal villus. I think it looks like the inside of a tentacle, even though I've never seen the inside of a tentacle. I imagine that I have an illness that slowly turns me into an octopus.

I'm completely unconscious during the gastroscopy, even though the general anaesthetic is light and short in duration. You did so well swallowing the gastroscopy, says the doctor. I'm not sure if I should say thank you, as I don't remember any of it, neither the swallowing or the anti-swallowing. I'm not certain I ever spat it out. But during an exhibition a few years later I see a video of a sword swallower and I have to run out on the street, retching.

The pearl diver has one of the little octopus arms (or is it a mouth) between her lips. Her mouth is open; it hasn't been forced open, but plays softly and freely with the tentacle. She has opened doors and gates and cavities and holes and let out all the fantasies inside. Maybe the octopi have manifested as an inversion of herself, but with this inversion she is also connected to the sea, the universe and eternity. Magically she has turned inside into outside and is caressed by her own intestines and organs, gels and fluids, bones and tentacles.

This is where magic takes over for logic. Don't try to follow me, just close your eyes, like the pearl diver. The octopi have emerged from the water, but her organs have emerged from her body too. The body is strung out on the beach now, and the ocean waves and molluscs are washed into and over her. Because they are her, have come from deep inside her, they can give and receive, they can touch her entire inside all at once, caress every single taste receptor. They participate in this infinite beat, flow with the jet stream and inside the spiral that is the innermost and darkest space. The inner outer space. The pearl diver lights lamppost after lamppost, line after line, dot after dot, in her own cosmos.

It's those frictions, this spark, that let in the imagination, that slowly stretch and connect all the gentle, impossible places. This is where I can say: imagine *Puberty* and the shadow around her body as the pearl diver and the octopi on the beach. Imagine that the shadow is a glowing, black organ that stretches out of her body, fusing inside and outside, darkness and glow, fury and joy, her hatred and mine. This is where I can say: imagine the Southerner's soft consonants and vowels, like when they say *hate* like *hadår* (or *Father* like *Fadær*), imagine how this softer language stretches like amphibian, salty tentacles from further down in the deep, down in the sea, the throat, the body, the underground, the magical dimensions.

These are the associations that white honesty erases, scrubbing them along its sheepback rocks. They can only be resurrected

174

in the underground. This is what I wanted to write to you, in a language that love couldn't summarise.

Tell me, in your darkness, in your ocean, am I ever there? Have we ever reached each other?

The Pixels

We're back where we started, in the camcorder universe, in the black metal bonus material. We see spruces, forest floor, grey sky. The camera movement has just made the forest sway and flicker as Nocturno Culto or Fenriz walks along the path, I don't remember which one. He's no longer in the frame. I've just scribbled something in the film's overcrowded side panel, and as I did so I briefly paused the video. We're now watching a still without people, a quarter-of-a-second loop with only nature, swirling trees, blurred tree trunks and vague clouds.

Here, the primitive digital camera technology meets subculture's low resolution. If we zoom further in on the image we won't see more detail. We can't see snowflakes shaken off the blurred branches or the difference between the bark and the wood inside it. We can't see the actual curves, the elasticity of the branches. The image is flat and pixelated, an unreal representation of reality. The file data doesn't bother with fidelity to nature, with gravity's pull or the associations of the treetops' upward growth. The only thing reproduced of this exaggerated colour contrast is an ambiguous chaos of black and white. The frame lacks nuance, yet deep down in the roots of subculture, in the network and seeding speed between the nerds, the fans and the enthusiasts, sending the file from machine to machine. The only thing we can zoom ourselves into is our own fantasy. Only I can supply these pixels with my own.

We're in a different image now. It's almost identical to the still, but this isn't from the Darkthrone DVD. This is a picture I've taken. We're not in 1993, but in 1998. The photograph is from a practice session with the metal band I'm in; we've probably attempted to record a music video late at night, but I'm not the one filming, of course. I've just photographed the place we've been, that's why there are no people in this image, only a clearing with a narrow path through the snow and some trees lit up by torches or the front lights of a car. You can just make out foot-prints next to each other on the dark snow under the trees. Apart from that, the image is coarse and underexposed, the snow is grey and all colours between the trees are erased, all of them black and dark grey. Only the contours of the treetops are visible against the sky.

I have a lot of these pictures of Southern forests, taken when I was in college, and I've seen a lot of similar motifs on Terese's old disks and from other black metal videos and band pictures from the '90s. In these photos it's always winter, and there are always the same trees, spruce and pine, the same sections of forest canopy. The pictures are never realistic; there's always too much movement or too little focus to give the sensation that anything's been captured. Branches, snow, stones and white-hot sky bleed into each other. I don't understand why I always take these kinds of pictures, test shots without people, the lighting far too dim, and the resolution too low. I have no interest in learning photography, not while I'm in college. My pitiful images are doomed to end up in the recycling bin on one of the school computers. But for some reason I keep doing it anyway, continue to use my terrible photography skills to document things that seem unnecessary. I continue to be pulled toward something, the bad, the empty and unreal.

A series of these images are emerging now, both stills and unused test-photographs. They are so similar they can almost be pieced together like a jigsaw puzzle, to form a continuous forest. But only just. Together they form a chaotic landscape, a crushed forest. It's not nature, or a reproduction of nature, that these images seek. These images want to destroy what we've been taught is reality. It's as if we're attempting the same thing, in different places, in different times, me and Darkthrone and lots of other teens. As if we're zooming into the darkness, into the silent letters, looking for a place that doesn't exist.

Look at this place here . . . in one of the pictures . . . and look at it here, in the next one. We're back in one of my document-ation images. It's impossible to see where it was shot – Fevik, Austre Moland, Nedenes, Groos?

Here, the real place doesn't exist anymore, just as Nocturno Culto doesn't exist in the frame of that first still. The only thing left is an impossible place.

We're in the eye of the camera. This graphic landscape has never been christened. It has no time or history; there was no Middle Ages here, no Reformation. No charismatic movement. There are only digital points, viruses and swirling canopies. The only possible conversion is the one I have done to my documentation photos, from MP4 to MP3, MOV, AVI, PNG, PDF, JPEG.

This place knows nothing of God. It's a screenshot, a series of moments, frozen and compressed from nature to JPEG. It does not know Holy Scripture. It does not know how to pronounce the ecclesiastical. No Christians see trees fall in this digital forest, and no god sees them, either. This is no man's land and no god's land. This is lowbrow, low-quality footage, hidden deep in the undergrowth of the cosmic internet. If this picture had any Christian content, or a parish centre nearby, it has been compressed out in the digitalisation. It's free, pagan, and it doesn't care. This is the bonus material of the South.

I want to be in a place like that in 1998, when I overhear recess prayer meetings organised for myself and other lost souls, when I'm in my witch's den trying not to hear the lyrics on the metal records I've borrowed, or when I wonder what the hell black metallers were thinking when they started burning beautiful stave churches instead of working their way through the premises of the Free Church, Betania and Salem and Filadelfia, plastered up and down the town streets with their tiny windows and creaking floors, sort of spying on us as we walk past, gluing shut the Southern spirit and mouth. I'm so sick of being a soul that can be converted or improved or healed, or that's dangerous and needs to be stopped from contaminating others. Give me a salvation break, I'm exhausted. I want to be in a place where I don't have anything to hate; I want to *be* that place, a place that can't be manipulated, conversed or converted. I want to be a thing, a series of things, things without religious potential. I want to be out of God's reach.

In school I'm never allowed to be that place. I imagine it's because I enjoy hating too much. I'm too fond of transgression. But now, twenty years after college, when I turn the screen toward Venke and Terese and we watch the black metal bonus material together, we sink into the undergrowth, and we choose the camera over the trees, or we choose the black and white trees over the real and green ones. We look past and into the patterns. We don't stop the movement, but let it continue, like an eternal scroll down the black whirling branches. We choose the pixels.

Listen to the MP3 buzz from the fan in the computer. It whispers a heathen psalm.

2

THE FOREST

A film

We open on a long scene from the middle of a film. A group of girls, maybe a school class, are on a forest hike. This is the first time that we join them outdoors. Our initial focus lingers on the girls as they walk through the forest landscape. Some of them are outdoorsy types and focused, and others more skittish and giggly. Everyone has brought typical hiking gear, back-packs, rolled-up mats, water bottles and flasks. They talk about previous hikes, about things they've brought and animals they've spotted. They wear sensible clothes, a lot of them are in hiking boots, and we watch them step over grass and rocks, pass through thickets and over fences. As the girls go deeper and deeper into the forest, we see less of them; they pop up erratically in between close-ups and long takes of nature, and the forest gradually takes over as the main character in the scene. We realise that the actors playing the girls are changing all the time, and always seem a little unfamiliar to us on reappearance, even though they are still addressed with the same five or six names. The forest pulls everything in and makes everything part of itself.

This forest is all forests. It alternates between heather clinging to rock faces, and tall Sitka spruces North American rainforests, and Eastern Norwegian marshland with fog and tall grass. The forest moulds itself around the girls. More than something inanimate passed through by something living, the landscapes come to the humans and change their consciousness and form. Forest and humans are made equals: the girls walk through a transformable landscape, but they are also part of the transformation.

The girls always wear the same clothes, even though the people inside them change. There are no constant faces here, only figures, exchangeable frames for the forest content.

Shots of animals, big and small, pausing and breathing rapidly in and out through their nostrils; it's as if the girls are taking the form of different beasts as they walk through the woods. All living beings are connected and belong together, become each other. Mushrooms and flowers stretch toward the hiking boots, the hooves and the paws that trample the landscape.

We hear individual voices ask each other very banal, mundane questions followed by quite long intervals of silence. For example:

ANNA: Carole, are you coming?
CAROLE: I've got a blister, wait up.

It's impossible to differentiate between the calcified trees and twisted, scorched stone boulders in the dry desert forest they walk through. The sun blinks as it shines through the fossils, and in the next moment it shines through the foliage of huge spider plants clawing into coastal cliffs, before we move to high mountain thickets and after that gradually down to a windswept

evergreen forest, and later to cacti and crystalline stone formations, as if the girls have been walking in circles. Dead desert
forest curves around them.

IVY: Where did we put the water?

Big, oak trees, green-leaved and eternal, seem to watch the
girls. In the next moment the sky drizzles and the leaves have
gone yellow and red, falling to the ground.

ANNA (looking at a compass that doesn't resemble a
    compass so much as a small digital sundial): In Carole's
    backpack.

They stop by a brook and fill their water bottles.
Beyond the brook the landscape opens up into wide plains.
The girls walk through grass and wildflowers, and around their
feet blood and/or other fluids drip on the flowers and the grass.
Gradually, the forest reveals increasingly vivid bodily formations to us, as if it's sending a message to the girls or trying to
mirror them. A series of trees look like twisted bodies with arms
that shake their fists at the sky. A mountain crevice in the
distance looks like a vagina. The girls step into it and disappear,
as if we can't follow them in there. Faint noises can be heard
from deeper and deeper inside the mountain, while the edges of
the crevice seem to twitch almost imperceptibly every time a
noise is heard.
Out on the other side of the mountain the sound of running

water can be heard. Two of the girls, TERESE and VENKE, squat next to each other, pissing. You see their butts and the piss that streams across dry dirt and flint.

VENKE (TO TERESE): How old were you when you kissed someone for the first time?

TERESE: Um . . . Thirteen. You?

VENKE: Twelve.

TERESE: Why?

VENKE: I was just wondering.

TERESE: What was the kiss like?

VENKE: Embarrassing.

TERESE: Same. And wet. I didn't know people were that wet.

VENKE: I remember that I was really keen and just went for it. I remember the sound of teeth against teeth, that bone sound. I'd forgotten about teeth.

TERESE: You think about the lips and dread the tongue, but forget the teeth.

VENKE: It's kind of like the first time you hear someone get knocked out. That whipping noise that films teach you, it doesn't exist. Only skeleton.

TERESE: The sound of life and death.

The sound of peeing continues.

TERESE and VENKE grab each other's hands to pull themselves up to a standing position, and move on in an autumnal landscape with fiery colours and afternoon sun blushing through the canopies. They walk up a hill, help each other carry the backpacks,

then they tumble down again, without the backpacks,

play with stuff they've brought with them, a bottle of water, a kerosene stove,

and perhaps something they definitely didn't bring, a volley-ball or a cabbage,

they play, faintly ecstatic,

but underneath this cheerfulness the mood is deeply euphoric in a more mystical way

they are changed by the landscape

they are part of it

they have already disappeared.

The girls take a break.

The colours change from blood-red to Norwegian green-black, that spruce green,

those trees that are always green, but with black, sort of, under-neath

like that '90s hair dye that was red, but with black underneath.

Dusk falls. VENKE and TERESE are seen sleeping in the forest; VENKE sucks on a tuft of her own hair, as if she is administering her own imaginary oxygen or nibbling on herself.

It's completely dark. Only forest and animal sounds. Some sounds seem real, others more abstract. A spider crawls over a blade of grass, and the little legs trample the blade with a violent and metallic ring, like the sound of an electroacoustic piece of music.

The black and the white whisper in distinct tones (overdub).

The horizon is black and white.

A cosmic but crawling and creeping soundscape is heard alongside this text:

SONG: (Darkthrone, in the distance):
Over peaks and through the thickets
Through this evil murky wood
Die like a warrior, head on a tree
Slash the flesh. Needles skin deep.

SONG: (interpretation of Darkthrone, in the distance)
Over stumps and through the leaves
An evil sea of mist deceives
Hidden words on murky waves
Sink into the moor's embrace
Lines that stretch horizon-long
Snare insanity through song
Shrouding all in fog of death
Sounds of white bone on the breath

Then it's pitch-black and sound is all there is.

The sounds come from a tape recorder that plays large expanses of organ notes. The long veil of echo from the notes spreads across the night sky in every direction. These expansive notes are cut off abruptly, crumbling into the ticking sound of a

Geiger counter, the way it ticks if it's placed near a ceramic salt shaker dyed with uranium oxide. Then the sound gets more defined, it verges on the sound of an old-fashioned modem that is connecting to the internet, or maybe an old printer; the sound is dimmed, but in the space between the abstract and the concrete is the possibility of infinity, and through tight hollows between little machines lined up next to each other, even the smallest strange spaces insist on infinity.

Then it's dawn, first astronomical, then civilian, and finally the common dawn.

As the forest slowly brightens around them, VENKE and TERESE, now played by the same actors all the time, are shown sleeping in formations around different natural objects, as if they have been arranged that way by the forest. The pictures resemble Valie Export's pictures.

VENKE is seen sleeping wrapped around a spruce.

TERESE sleeps in a hollow in a clearing, her butt nestled deep down, legs and arms stretched out to either side.

VENKE is on a beach by a little pond, legs in the water.

TERESE rests on a big, round stone, belly down and legs and arms dangling on either side.

VENKE is in an oak tree, sleeping with legs and arms embracing a thick branch.

When TERESE wakes up it's dark again, as though a whole day has passed without them waking. Only the moon lights up the sky. The forest doesn't look like the one we last saw VENKE asleep in; now it's a spruce forest near the timberline. TERESE looks around, calls out faintly. We don't hear her yell for VENKE, but we hear the echoes of the calls.

VENKE isn't far away, and we hear the echo as she yells back
HI, TERESE.

TERESE and VENKE find each other, laugh. Spend a little while packing up their stuff, look around,

VENKE: We've lost the others.
TERESE: Yes. When did we last see them?
VENKE: I don't remember. Last night?
TERESE: We'll have to find them again, I suppose.

For an entire day, TERESE and VENKE walk through the forest, from when the sun is still rising till it's evening again. They keep moving and are calm, not distressed or at a loss for what to do. At first the landscape continues to change, as if they were crossing continents and wandering for months, and the forest opens and closes, becomes big mountains and narrow valleys and then is suddenly completely flat, with red sandy mountains in the distance. Then the forest stabilises in the form of a Norwegian spruce forest, but the images change. We see an increasing number of landscape close-ups. Buzzing insects fly in and out of hollows in tree trunks above the girls, and farther up, birds float with extended wings and limp thin feet. Even farther up you can make out the sky, the moon and the stars, sometimes just a little patch, sometimes a great sea of them.

TERESE and VENKE are sweaty and dirty and sleepy, they wipe their foreheads, panting,

but at the same time the mood becomes more erotically charged.

They snort and moan,

touch different kinds of trees as they walk,

pick berries and mushrooms that they eat, and drink water from streams,

stick their fingers through grass and into openings in tree trunks,

dig out and chew bark and resin,

they see Roosevelt elk and roes cross marshes,

bats flying across the sky,

blue hares and red foxes running across the path.

Coyotes laugh, and wolves howl.

The girls begin to communicate with the animals and with nature,

as if they've eaten toadstools and begun to hallucinate.

They call for the hare and the fox,

they lie down in moss and lichen and let the wolf lick their faces,

they roll in plants, red, green, gold, yellow,
they disappear more and more into the landscape
and return like breathing, or like a children's game

At times they vanish from sight, and we return to a few images of
the forest, without VENKE and TERESE. We see the piss dry on the
earth,
the blood dry on the flowers
something black trickling onto the red
black blood mixing with the red

All colours slowly fade to black, in the way everything turns black
and disappears when the sun sets.

Another day begins.

VENKE continues to walk through the forest; TERESE is heard
behind her. Close-ups.
Is it the same day, or the next day?

Suddenly new steps are heard, and VENKE crashes into someone
else, an unfamiliar person, ŚMIERĆ. We see the collision in close-
ups, it's embarrassing and weird, and they nudge a lot of places
on each other's bodies: hand against hip, hip against hip, belly
against breasts, cheek against cheek.
VENKE and ŚMIERĆ both end up on the ground. TERESE bends
over and puts her hand on VENKE.

TERESE: Are you OK?

VENKE (rubs hand on knee): Yeah.

TERESE and VENKE look at ŚMIERĆ, who is dressed entirely in black, with a tattered leather jacket, leather trousers, spikes on his arms and corpse paint on his face, looking a little worn out.

TERESE: Hi, are you OK?

ŚMIERĆ: Nie rozumiem, co mówisz.

TERESE: Oh, sorry . . . English? Are you okay?

ŚMIERĆ (very broken): Ah! Yes, okay.

VENKE: What are you doing out here?

ŚMIERĆ: Oh . . . um . . . photo shoot.

VENKE: Photo shoot?

ŚMIERĆ gesticulates to signal air guitar riffs and bad growling.

ŚMIERĆ: Photo shoot with, you know, Norway forest. Black metal.

VENKE: Black metal band! Where is your photo shoot?

ŚMIERĆ: Um . . . I . . . up this way . . . no, that way . . .
no . . . don't know. I am . . . lost.

VENKE: Oh.

ŚMIERĆ: Yes.

TERESE looks at ŚMIERĆ, who shrugs, and then looks at VENKE. She wipes a little corpse paint from her cheek that has rubbed off on her from ŚMIERĆ.

TERESE: You had a little . . .

The three of them continue through the forest landscape, which now appears to be rooted in a Southern hilly marshland, somewhere within that magical triangle of Southern villages, Arendal, Froland and Grimstad. Dark spruce, ponds, and blueberry heather surround the hikers. TERESE and VENKE hike competently, reconnoitring at the clearings and on top of hills, stopping ŚMIERĆ when they sense a moose or a fox or hear other noises. ŚMIERĆ follows them; he's more bewildered and wearing a spikey jacket and belt and boots that aren't suited for hiking. He gradually smudges his makeup all over his face and breathes deeply. Sometimes he hums a little to himself, other times he just looks desperate.

During a break the three of them stop. ŚMIERĆ is whirling around, as if he's a little anxious, looking for ticks or insects before he sits down on a stump. Brushes ants from his shoe.

TERESE: (to Venke, whispering faintly, but excitedly): He's in a black metal band!

VENKE: Isn't that sort of 1991, though?

In some frames we no longer see the people, we just wobble through the forest, seeing it from the people's perspective. Gradually the sight line is lowered, with the canopies higher and higher up in the sky, until we see from the perspective of a rat.

The music over this hiking scene starts as a standard atmospheric black metal intro, with synths and maybe a gong, that extends over time, never becoming a song. The forest swirls past as the volume gradually increases and the drone sounds are slightly displaced and disrupted, as if we've entered a zone where electrical equipment doesn't work, or we're on a Skype call with a poor connection. The disruptions and the dissonances of the music shift over to the forest itself; it begins to flicker and grow more and more pixelated. VENKE and TERESE look around; they notice it, too. For a long time, VENKE stares right at us, has she glimpsed something? Then it's peaceful and quiet again. A little darker, but otherwise unchanged.

The three of them continue on their hike. ŚMIERĆ starts to look tired, sweaty and scared. The girls take his tote bag, decorated with an upside-down pentagram, and take turns carrying it. They don't look tired, but perhaps seem more detached, as if they sense something.

The music changes now, into sounds that we can't quite fit into a genre. We're in a new place, where we can make connections we don't understand. The forest has done something to us, we've forgotten where we came from, forgotten that there are machines and clever indie pop music and noise and traffic and hard synthetic sounds and soapy hard-plastic products. We've disintegrated entirely, into little prehistorical jellyfish cubes, and find comfort in everything that seems organic. Blood and menstruation and shit and piss and rotting fungus seem safer than the gleaming and alien things we don't understand.

The three wanderers are about to finish a break in a forest clearing. ŚMIERĆ looks calmer, but sweaty and twisted, as if he's on his way into a trance. The girls are a little worried about him.

VENKE: Have some water.
ŚMIERĆ: No, no.

They start to walk again. ŚMIERĆ gets up, then collapses. TERESE and VENKE turn around, sit down on either side of him, place a rolled-up jacket under his head.

> VENKE: What's wrong?
> ŚMIERĆ (quiet): Aaaaaaaaaaaa.
> VENKE: Are you in pain?
> ŚMIERĆ: Aaaaaaaaaaaa.
> TERESE: Tell us what's wrong!
> ŚMIERĆ: Aaaaaaaaaaa.

TERESE and VENKE try to help: they make a bed of moss and fabric they strip from the backpack; they undress him and start to wash his body. The water droplets they pour over him make crystal noises like the sounds from a wind chime, but just evaporate on his skin. ŚMIERĆ continues to chant AAAAAAAAAA, looking straight ahead, as if he knows what's happening.

TERESE puts her hand on ŚMIERĆ's belly to clean it, but then retracts it swiftly. We notice a round shape on his belly, a little bulge that grows gradually bigger.

TERESE puts her hand on VENKE's. A thin white membrane covers their eyes like an inner eyelid. In a trance they continue to wash his belly around the bulge and the water runs down the side of his body, outlining its contours in water, like a chalk outline of a hand.

Slowly his makeup is transformed from corpse paint to an Edvard Munch face,

which is then made up into an entirely white face again,
as if dipped in sugar or crystals,
and then into a face without makeup
but also without characteristics, without eyes, nose or mouth
perhaps totally in line with what we recognise as human,
with only generic orifices
or is that just what a face looks like when the makeup is
removed and we look too closely?

VENKE's and TERESE's faces change, too. The skin around their eyes swells and becomes red and sore, as if their eyelids have become lips, and their irises are split into little kaleidoscopic colour particles.

Finally brownish black goo starts oozing from all of ŚMIERĆ's orifices. It's sometimes a little lumpy, then smoother, more watery.

The girls begin to smear the gunk over his body, initially trying to get rid of it, but later just to make a bit of a mess. It starts to gently etch his skin, like oil slowly brought to a boil.

Gunk begins to bubble under the skin around the bulge on his belly.

ŚMIERĆ breathes quickly and closes his eyes in pain. The girls demonstrate birth breathing with pursed lips, which he attempts to mimic.

The girls study the bulge on the belly. It moves as a finger under a carpet would. They start to gather lichen and moss and leaves and flowers and arrange their haul at the bottom of ŚMIERĆ's belly.

The thin flower stalks and lichen flakes merge into thicker amphibian folds around the bulge. Slowly we realise that they form an opening, a vagina. Like a sculpture, or a piece of clothing they're designing. When the girls remove their hands, you can see a hint of movement from the end pieces of the folds, like little tentacles.

Then the girls press their fingers against the vagina, which slowly begins to open. Brown-black gunk gushes over their hands.

TERESE shifts her hands up toward ŚMIERĆ's face and places a twig carefully between his teeth, so he can bite on it. She starts to breathe in his face, strong quick breaths that he tries to mimic. In the meantime VENKE sticks first one finger into the hole to feel it, then two, and then her arm deep in, as if up a cow's rectum. TERESE carries on doing the birth breathing. They shout.

VENKE and TERESE: PUSH!

ŚMIERĆ pushes and screams a long HHHHHHHHHHHHHHH-HH. Black blood gunk doesn't gush anymore but pulses calmly as it flows from the vagina, continuing in beautiful lava-like streams down the sides of the belly, over the crotch and back to nature. TERESE's and VENKE's tongues swim in clear spit, and the drool runs down their chins as they work.

TERESE has turned back toward VENKE who with some effort manages to extract a small, round, white egg as ŚMIERĆ pushes one last time. All three enter into a deeper trance with the egg between their hands.

TERESE: We found it.
VENKE: In a hole we made with our own hands. I was inside.

TERESE: What was it like in there?

VENKE: Warm and soft, red and black, white and yellow.

TERESE: Egg white and egg yolk.

VENKE: I didn't have access, but I wasn't expelled.

Slowly the three of them come out of the deepest part of the trance. VENKE rolls her head lightly from side to side, as if she's stretching. TERESE carefully changes her sitting position. They look at each other.

It's unclear who says:

I just felt like I've gotten so close to you now, am I nuts? Maybe it's the forest, maybe it's VENKE, maybe TERESE, maybe it's me telling you.

TERESE and VENKE lay the egg, which glistens and glitters and radiates light as if from a flashlight or an iPhone, on ŚMIERĆ's chest. He is tired and happy. He pets the egg and laughs.

But then he jerks and disappears into a trance again. We watch his hair and skin start to melt, and the magical vagina starts rotting. ŚMIERĆ is still all smiles, but his breathing grows irregular.

Then he slowly becomes grainier and grainier
      like a picture that is corrupted as it's copied again and again
      like a picture that's resampled and resampled in gradually
lower resolution
      until he's completely invisible and blurred.

All the while TERESE and VENKE whisper, this time in Norwegian: Where are you going? Don't be scared, relax. Go in, but not toward the egg white. See, do you see the other colours? There are so many more colours. Go to them. Do you see the black, the black yolks? Go to the yolks. Go to them. Happy death.

TERESE and VENKE (hum):
Over whites and through the yolk
Looms the shrouded song of death
Waves make for a murky cloak
Sounds of white bone on the breath

ŚMIERĆ has now completely disappeared into a bigger and bigger pool of black gunk that bubbles and seethes. Only the skeleton and the rotting vagina, the phantom hole, are left.

The egg is wobbling on the edge, as if it considers jumping back into the hole,

but the hole gradually closes, bit by bit, like a seam,

and finally melts into the black puddle,

which seethes and boils, reducing into a black blot of gruel.

Two hands are placed on the gruel.

A Satanic pact between you and me.

They start to pick up and break apart the skeleton pieces. After a lot of back and forth and with the aid of both teeth, elbow grease and crushing stomps, they manage to break them up and arrange them into a new form.

Afterward they lie on either side of the bone sculpture and exhale, relieved.

From above you can see two girls resting on their backs, hands stretched out across a white bone mass in the shape of an upsidedown cross, with the skull at the top and the egg in the middle where the lines cross each other.

Slowly the bones, too, disappear into the earth, or the earth emerges up from the ground in the form of little ants, dragging the pieces down into the underground.

TERESE and VENKE (hum):
Sounds of white shell on its breath

The egg is left alone again on the ground, wobbles.

The egg trembles even more,
   The egg is about to fall,
   now the egg falls
   into TERESE's hand
   VENKE puts her hand outside TERESE's.
   TERESE puts her other hand around the other side of the egg.
   VENKE then puts her other hand around that one.

VENKE: One, two, three!

On 'three' the girls lift the egg and put it in Venke's backpack. They wrap their clothes and a towel around it.

The membranes slide open and disappear from VENKE's and

TERESE's eyes. They look at each other, they look at the egg nested in the backpack.

As the girls pack, the last pixelated remains of ŚMIERĆ drain down into the stones and moss and earth, down toward the underground and the deepest roots, like cream absorbed into skin, penetrating the layers of meat and bone and marrow. Soon the body and its shape have completely disappeared, and only a little stripe of black sand remains on the brown earth, like a tiny lava-stream fossil, a burnt-out witch's bonfire.

The girls begin to walk again, slowly. The anxiety of the entire forest is dominated by the fragility of the egg. The girls monitor the egg constantly, hold the egg, warm the egg, rock the egg.

Their hands are visible on the egg, they stroke it, warm it, wrap it up in jumpers, moss and plants. They roll it carefully up hill-tops and pass it to each other when they have to climb a fence or step over a brook. TERESE cleans the egg with a damp cloth and VENKE puts it on her chest, as if nursing it. They sleep with the egg between them, their upper bodies naked. They lie awake looking at the egg in the dark, in the flickering light from the fire's licking flames.

Sometimes one of them wakes up while the other continues to sleep, and only when the first one falls asleep does the other wake. Without knowing it, they push the same nightmare back and forth between each other: one where the egg has rolled too close to the fire and been hardboiled.

It's light again. The hiking continues, through thickets and over tree stumps, further into the Southern waves of hills and marshes. But the forest is gradually disappearing from the surroundings, as if the egg radiated a new light replacing everything happening around it. The girls walk through brushwood and rain, over fences and down slopes, but the colours of the landscape are being rubbed out; first the brightest colours, then the softer shades, until it looks like we're in a pencil sketch or a written-in notebook. Finally the lines fade and are washed white, and we move blindly along the margin, hesitant, as though we're snow-blind after staring at the egg's shell too long.

There are no shapes left in the picture anymore. Trees and hills aren't visible. Nature has been transformed into vague memories of nature. Only VENKE and TERESE are visible, and only barely; we see them as a baby perceives contours or bold shapes, like a tongue that moves under the skin in the jaw. The egg is perceived only dimly and as a negative, as what's held in the girl's folded arms. VENKE is seen clenching white-knuckled hands around nothing, or maybe the egg, but TERESE's hands, too, cling to something, hold something over her chest.

Then the sound of the walking and of the forest fades out, we no longer hear the girls breathe or sniff, talk or shout. We no longer hear twigs snap, or shoes squishing on moss, or birds singing or insects buzzing. Maybe it happened gradually: the sounds became more and more electric and manipulated and now the birds and the bumblebees and VENKE and TERESE have been replaced by synthetic effects and algorithms, or maybe someone abruptly switched off the sound.

Perhaps we're on our way through a portal, where everything is toned down and rubbed out, cleansed, restarted.

The only sound left is the sound of my voice. This sound is everything, it comes from all directions at the same time, as if the mouth that speaks is around us, as if we've been swallowed by the forest itself. The sound is the sound of the text in my book, this book, read inside your own head.

We strain to understand the whispered words, but most of the sounds feel as though they have no meaning; they're only a physical process, airy vowels and tiny consonants that rub against the mouth. The sounds of the voice have become abstract; they're vaguely reminiscent of tingling, little grains of sand in an otherwise white and infinite room, like the sound of an old Geiger counter.

Each phrase from the voice is followed by a silence that disappears into the white forest. Every sequence full of sound has an empty twin, a moment of nothing, a negative. The silence emerges like a reflex, a blink, without associations, without content, as if every sound has been directed at something else and waits for an answer from the other side of the wasteland.

Upon encountering the light, the shape of the egg has been rubbed out or inverted, and the egg now beams so powerfully that we can't look straight at it: the egg is everything.

Form is the thing in us that stretches, that pushes the boundaries between us, against us, creating the sensation of intimacy. Here in the white forest, feet are one with the ground they step on, bodies pass straight through trees, the bark and skin tickle each other, their movements synchronised. White mushroom caps growing from white sand stretch directly into our bodies, soft like porridge. We don't know if we're on our way through something or if we're stuck. We don't know if we're alive. All boundaries are rubbed out, and nothing is impenetrable anymore.

Or perhaps these descriptions don't describe the forest; perhaps they describe our own resistance to it. To describe is also to construct form and perspective; it's the reflex of mortal dread. Could language be used for something else? Aren't there other reasons to write? If we let go of the descriptions, will we discover that we're no longer moving at all, since we already exist within everything in here? We've given up shapes, our own shells and components and we're back in a flow, that gelatinous substance that ruled the earth before the harder minerals, rock types, skeletons and shells came into existence. This could be the beginning, the egg white, the original place, the original life.

I wanted to meet you in this place. I wanted to meet you where we leak, where we're almost nothing, here in someone else's story. A place where I have given up almost everything: body, self, clarity, every component. I wanted to meet you here and talk to you about love, about bonds between people, about form and content within those bonds. About how they glitter like a shortcut to something human through the dimensions; I wanted to grab it, hold it, give it space and listen to it. I wanted to meet you, but it only exists in flashes, at moments, in little eggs.

Are you here?

Pale, faint sound waves have begun to oscillate in the white light now. Blurred electronic drone images replace the silence

with sonic form. We sense that something is happening somewhere else, that the sound of it has been brought to us from places
we can only hear, as if from behind an impenetrable wall. Our
ears stretch and travel through time and space faster than sight or
body. We're getting nearer all the time.

The girls come out into a clearing in the white forest, where
the white light gradually dims until we can make out trees and
grass in the background again. First we see them only as contours,
as rough pencil sketches, the preliminary stages of a painting.
Then the empty sections between the edges are filled in with
pale colours from a thick brush.

The wind is blowing hard. The music has gotten louder, and
the sound waves, along with the sound of the wind blowing, fill
us up. They fill us up, just as the gradually brighter colours start
to fill in the sketches of trees and grass and sky. The ears and the
image and the eggshell vibrate.

VENKE, TERESE and the egg look around at their new surroundings. The landscape appears teeming and dramatic compared
with the sedate forest and white light the girls have just travelled
through. The place is both familiar and unfamiliar, a harsh
Southern forest, estranged. A pale new moon hangs crooked
between the clouds in the sky, above the birch crowns and the
moors. The egg is in someone's hands and gleams in the
moonlight.

Initially the girls think they've arrived at the family farm of
Arne Myrdal, the leader of the People's Movement Against
Immigration. But then they understand that they are at Knut
Hamsun's farm in Nørholm, south of Grimstad, where Hamsun

tried to write and cultivate the forest floor like Isak Sellanrå in *The Growth of the Soil*. Maybe Hamsun believed in magic, too contaminated by the Southern spirit, he wanted to make his own art real. Maybe Hamsun was interested in the spirits of the soil, too. Twenty years later he was a Nazi, and seventy-five years after that I raised my hand in Norwegian class to say his *Pan* was an insult to the brain.

At the far end of the clearing is a little white house. It looks like a summer house; it's old and has thin walls. It's Hamsun's writing lodge. The paint is flaking, the windowpanes are fragile and thin, and water damage has cracked the windowsills and wall panels.

The girls walk slowly through the clearing toward the entrance on the side of the house. The door is cracked open, just enough to fit a small egg. They climb the little stone stairs slowly.

Inside the house it's terribly dark, and VENKE and TERESE are just sketches of insignificant shapes on a wood-panel background and the old hallway pictures. They glide slowly through one room and then a small passage to get to the main room where you can barely make out a couple of flickering black wax candles.

A corner is turned and VENKE, TERESE and the egg are in a living room, where their eyesight gradually adjusts to the dim lighting. The room is almost empty, with panelled walls and faint shadows of old-fashioned summer furniture in the corner. Along one wall you can just make out the remains of a fireplace, but where the flue should be is a patch of black, blurred mass, framed by dirt and polystyrene packaging painted black.

The rest of the girls, all those who appeared earlier in the story, have returned and are standing in the middle of the room, spread out around a chalk circle on the wooden floor. They look up and smile softly, and VENKE and TERESE smile back, as if they've all been waiting for each other.

The egg is heavy in VENKE's and TERESE's hands as they transport it into the room, past the other girls, who stand just outside of the chalked circle that divides the dark wood flooring, making an inside and an outside. Then the other girls are allowed to hold the egg, one after the other. The egg is passed between hands and through the room; it's constantly moving, floating along the perimeter of the circle, recognising its own shape and the five-pronged pentagram that's sketched inside the circle. It is weighed and caressed, floating through the room on a sea of fingers and skin. The egg moulds itself around each girl's body, and then it takes the bodies with it, lures them and beckons them further into the circle.

We watch the living room gradually brighten, and in the black webbing where the stairway should have been, we spot a small crevice that slowly begins to resemble a rotten orifice with shrivelled labia. A little loosened webbing has congealed on the edges. The light is still faint and casts numerous shadows of windowsills, planks and furniture, but a light like a UV light or a tanning salon bulb shines on the web and the opening.

The egg is in the middle of the circle. It floats along past the shapes. The music has become deafening, threatening the eardrums. Windowpanes vibrate. The shell's surface temperature rises.

The boiler is seething, the modem for the cosmic internet. Imitation smoke, which might be from a fire or a smoke machine, flows across the living room floor, and seeps in and out of the hole, as if, on the other side, a fire is breathing or someone is smoking a cigarette.

TERESE's and VENKE's hands are visible in the picture. The egg floats in their hands, or just above their hands.

With a lot of hubbub, the hands thrust the egg into the orifice.

The black labia slowly widen as the opening is enlarged.

The girls push themselves, head first, through the opening.

3

THE EGG

Let me see . . .

At first the darkness is all consuming and boundaries are insignificant. We don't know if we see out of or into our own bodies. We don't know if we're at one with everything, or if we're buried alive. Then we spot a few edges, shifting, or contours that gleam in light from an unknown source, or perhaps from the whites of our own eyes. The contours hurl themselves at us, forming geometric patterns through the dark, like a knife carving secret signs into black paper. We stretch our eyes into the patterns and see a brighter spot in the distance, above us. We get the feeling that we're underneath something, that above us there's a surface. With fingers and arms and legs we kick off to get up and out of the dark. It's the same movement: legs that kick off from underwater to rise up, and fingers pinched and flicked open across a screen or a touchpad to zoom out.

We zoom out. We're now in a digitised class photo. Behind the lined-up students is a vague background, that kind of generic wallpaper that's always put up for the backdrop of school photos – blue with cotton-white clouds, as if all the teens who have ever gone to school were angels in heaven . . . The room constructed in this photo has minimal content, little depth, and no sense of time. It's a room that denies us comfort, that doesn't let us be ourselves, as we've defined ourselves. The room makes room for something else, something flat, finalised and arranged, conventional. The students, the teacher, every item of clothing, the glasses and jewellery, all personal characteristics, everything is interchangeable. Every class photo could be any class photo.

The *class photo*, as photographic reproduction and genre, doesn't care about the teens in the photo. It doesn't depict who's had sex, or who would've had sex if they'd had the opportunity. It doesn't care about who speaks in tongues, who sings in metal bands, or who will march with the Nordic Resistance Movement twenty years later. The high-resolution bitmap graphics split people up into tiny little points, reproduce pimples and moles with supreme accuracy, but at the same time ignore us entirely as individuals, as sinners, as moral, judgemental and doomed beings. The image doesn't give a flaming fuck about the students' souls, or their mortality, or their grace or their misery. The photo says, Even Southerners are points and pigments. The photo speaks matter-of-factly, without magic or blasphemy.

Class 2B, 1998, it says in the bottom right corner, printed with thin white letters, like a stage-prop tombstone, *Class 2b were here.* There we are, submitting to the systems. We are perfectly arranged, wedged into the institutional pattern. We are evidence, lined up where the church and the school system naturally meet. We smile the wavering smile of conformity.

I'm the black-clad one in the top left corner. Around me are Christian and non-Christian classmates dressed in white, purple, red, green and pink. The girls wear low-rise mini-flare jeans.

They have long corkscrew curls or hair straightened with a flat-iron. Some of the boys have crew cuts, some wear their hair long, others keep it shoulder-length. Many are wearing knitted jumpers in grey, blue, and white Icelandic patterns. Some are lighter-skinned, others darker. Some have put on makeup, others not. Some look straight ahead, some glance at one another.

Look at the picture this way, and then look at it again.

It's impossible for an unknowing eye to spot the difference in our smiles, but at the moment this picture was taken, I've just said *fucking hell*, in the middle of the photo shoot. Half the class are about to stop smiling; they are about to look around for the sinner as they cautiously cross themselves and touch their hands to their hearts. A moment later everything will be defined, crossed, damned, forgiven and blessed. But right now, in this image, there is chaos; the students aren't sure what happened yet, who said the word. Sound is faster than comprehension, faster than what they call heart and soul and sin. Right now my voice could have come from any of my Christian classmates, a slip of the tongue, a Tourette's tic; that's why they react and why they are about to cross themselves. Everyone in the class is a potential sinner. The uncertainty is shapeless, even in the middle of this conformity; they themselves aren't exempt; the guilt includes everyone in the room and leaks from one thing to another. No one remains dry, everyone is defiled. Just as the most evangelical of them feel defiled when we're taught by the lesbian teacher: they fear that she'll lure them over to her side, that they will say what she says, that they'll become, or realise that they already are, like her.

The photo is stuck in this moment, in the uncertainty. It comprises us, compresses us, cranks up the pressure and the temperature. The whole image, this place, is a witches' Sabbath for teenagers.

In this moment there's hope. There's hope for transformation and magic. It's possible to interpret class photos differently. Maybe all of Class 2B, and every student from all Norwegian class photos, are actually standing there hating. Maybe we all hate the photographer, the angelic blue background, and the Christian Democratic People's Party's first government, and the royal family and the school nurse and the teachers and the charismatic pastors and the laughing gospel choir and God, and *What Would Jesus Do* and the rhythm and the tempo and the vocals and the consonants in that outdated creed.

And who am I? I'm the one honking outside reality, disrupting and cursing. I'm the one who flares up like a shadow behind others, threatening to paint over and darken the whole picture in misanthropic black. Blacking out the images is always a possibility, even though we usually choose the concealer and the powder when we want to make ourselves invisible. I'm the other option, the smouldering dome, the black steam from the occult fires of hatred. I am *Girls hating through centuries*, THE END.

Or maybe it's not THE END.

The most important thing about magic is obviously that it never ends. What's most important about magic is to create meeting places, so that later, others can stretch further into this artistic space. The desire to go there never ceases. This need to change, translate, transgress, transcend, smudge, it's never satisfied. We never stop hating. Hatred and hope don't change. Hatred and hope will continue to chime together and curse the world with its clearly articulated *h*-sounds.

The film script is finished, but the writing of the film continues anyway. I never stop writing. Writing happens in the margins; the future bonus material is written there. The word END, or FIN, or SLUTT in Norwegian, in white on a black screen, has always just meant YOU'RE WELCOME. It just means that the screen goes blank, that the film's images are swapped for an impenetrable black slate, a mysterious blank sheet which you yourself can continue writing on, or seep into. That's why I like films better than books: they end in black instead of white. The book's last blank pages always look like walking into a white cloud, the paper fibres are illusory optimism and total absorption, as if all the characters that were ever written into a book are angels in the sky.

The film's ending, as I originally wrote it, is my tribute to the fade to black, to transcendence in the dark as an alternative to the light. When the girls enter the black orifice of the writing lodge, it's me wanting to tamper with all the white, with the white sheet, the white silence and the white parish centres. I want to open up the Southern towns and reveal the darkness in there. This darkness should be both frightening and sensual, as if the South put two fingers inside its own body, pleasuring itself. In 1997, when I walk into an auditorium during a prayer meeting by mistake, the pastor is preaching about the dangers of *tampering with yourself.* To tamper: to finger, to pull at, destroy, manipulate. Smudging the Christian soul. A selfish sin, like the first text I hand my writing tutor, according to him, before I learn *from the outside, with insight.* Selfish, alienating and private, he says. Pitiful and primitive.

I never come to understand *from the outside, with insight.* But I understand that art can tamper with itself, with its own past, its own history, and create new bonds and new feelings. Now, after the film is finished, I think I can go further than when I wrote it. I dream of one last image in the film. This isn't an image I want to write into the document itself, not after the girls' hike through the white, invisible forest, the ritual in the writing lodge and the writing lodge's orifice. We've already reached the end, gone from the recognisable to the white, and then to the black. But still, I'm thinking about another scene, a new version of the end, a scene that's cut out of history even before it's written.

Let me show you the scene. We're back in 1998, for the last time, I promise. It's after the gig that my metal band and I play at the old parish centre, the venue that has been converted to a rock club, but not converted enough. We've left the room where the contours of tightly nailed-down crosses push into the walls, where the crocheted curtains are tangled together like folded hands, and the contours of the words 'Jesus lives' are still visible on the wall over the pool table. I have played a whole gig while nursing a suspicion that I've been tricked into attending another 'youth night' in a venue that's a Bible school in disguise, with the microphone stand resting in a hollow where the altar once was, the black-clad metal boys watching us, their hands stretched into the air in exactly the same way that hands stretch toward Jesus in praise and glossolalia.

Now my metal band, the two boys and I are on a forest trail, on our way to a churchyard and a church in the distance, to take a band photo. It's an early summer evening, midsummer solstice, and still completely light. The band stops between a few trees to take a picture here too, a test shot. All three line up. We stay here, as if this were a freeze frame, even though the wind ruffles my hair and my eyes blink.

The Southern forest where the boys and I are looks like the one surrounding Hamsun's old farm. Perhaps I'm looking at the writing lodge behind the camera as the test shot is taken. But the camera doesn't turn. Instead the frame and the band and I remain totally still as it slowly grows dark, from dusk to total misanthropic black.

Let's imagine that this scene is the end of the film, even though it isn't. Up until this point the film would have been pretty short, under an hour. This image could be spliced in afterward, keep running for a long time while the band's members, myself included, stand totally still and the wind rushes through our hair and the tree canopies. Three hours, maybe five, exactly the time it takes to go from day to night in the Norwegian summer. During the scene, as dusk approaches, unexpected details appear. I don't know if it's the image itself that changes, or if it's our watching that begins to change what we see, but through the dusk we notice that the guitarist in the band has Venke's hair and neck, and that the drummer perhaps shares some of Terese's facial features. The vocalist, me, has my black hair and black clothes, but maybe I've also got a new shadow drawn from my nostrils to the bow of my lip. Is it darkness that has thrown a shadow across my face, or is it a scar from a cleft lip?

At first the forest is quiet, only the odd bird chirping, but then you start to hear music far off. Maybe it's coming from the church at the end of the path, from behind the churchyard, or maybe it's being played deep inside the band members' bodies. This is what can be heard: A guitar playing fast riffs, distorted and buzzing, insect-like, and a drum beat with a timbre as deep as if it came from a mausoleum. The vocalist sings something slurred about hating, in Norwegian, maybe this: 'I love hating so much, the hatred burns, do you hear me?' Yeah! someone from the audience yells, because now we're hearing an audience too, from far off, through the music. Maybe you're the one yelling, maybe it's everyone.

After a while the music dissolves again until it's just reverberation, along with the summer winds making the leaves and grass rustle. Then it fades into the tempo of dusk itself and the scene continues until it's dissolved by darkness. First to melt into the shadow of the canopies and the surrounding trunks is the band. Finally, the sky and the faint contours of canopies surrounding us are also totally gone, black.

This is the easiest way to tamper with reality, the most primitive, the least costly, the most accessible gateway, cheaper and simpler than toilet paper. I imagine that we can meet here, you and I, as an audience, and watch our own places, the South, Norway, the forest, the band photo, disappear so slowly that we can't say exactly when the real forest has become a black, blank monochrome.

At some point we'll feel like we're hallucinating, that we see a colour that isn't really there, or the contours of a little black goat will appear next to me, and in that moment, when we no longer know if what we see is actual pixel information, fantasy, or texture on the inside of our own eyelids, the illusion of reality and the illusion of fiction melt into a joint place, an impossible place, where reality and fiction are only the extremities, the space in front of the capital letter and the full stop at the end of the long impossible sentence that we can write in between, together, inside the magical.

Are you there, in that last unwritten scene, in the dark?

Are you scrolling through the South now? Risør, Tvedestrand, Arendal, Grimstad, Lillesand? Are you zooming, kicking off with two fingers across the touchpad?

Dusk settles in so slowly and lasts for so long that we might have time to think the same things, breathe in time with each other, imagine the same images. Lines and dots appear in the black and join to form an image:

A pair of thighs glimpsed underneath a skirt's hem, with their moles and comedones, and if we study each point for long enough they form a constellation directing our gaze toward the deepest black hole. We go further and further into the room between the legs, between the lines, while the universe in there becomes steadily bigger and more expansive. Everything's in there.

A series of images fade in during the zoom:

Star map

World map

Older and older world maps where borders and accuracy shift and more and more imaginary kingdoms appear. We get farther and farther away from the mundane globe, and nearer and nearer Hy-Brasil and Atlantis.

A waffle segment with brown cheese spins in kaleidoscopic crystals. Waffles already have patterns, and through the kaleidoscopic lens every little square on the heart-shaped segment beams different coloured lights into the surrounding air, like mirror balls, freshly fried.

A group of witches dressed in padded coveralls stand in a circle on a marsh, singing loudly and energetically and with their whole bodies. Every voice is different, every voice breaks away from the melody in different places.

A quicker collage sequence begins, perhaps a roll of film with rips and holes:

A girl swims, seen through the kaleidoscope.

Blood, or pinkish-red foaming water, runs into the drain of a dirty sink.

A nebula slowly twists inward in a spiral.

White larvae, insects and butterflies stream out of a hole.

A needle shaft, a little thick, pushes into skin, then punctures and shoots through it.

A thumb is stuck in a mouth.

Jelly flung through air.

Fast movements through hyperspace.

A close-up of frozen pizza topping melting, like a blurrier and blurrier prehistoric world map of Norway's underground. Closer and closer to Hy-Brasil and Atlantis, in the shape of mythological bits of pepper.

A band, standing by a monument, toss their hair around in slow motion.

A waffle with jam is folded up and looks like blood-covered labia.

Marie Hamsun sits in a white hammock in a summer garden, Nørholm 1943.

Mashed potatoes topped with beets trembling in slow motion.

Body parts are displayed: abstract but sensual curves, one side of a lower leg, an arch, a spine, a close-up of an armpit with curly hair, the dip between collarbones, a wrist bone, an eye socket, an earlobe.

Labia open and close, letting out little drops of blood.

An eye cries or blinks.

A face speaks in tongues, coming extremely close, tears streaming from the eyes and nose, the edges of the mouth and chin wet from drool, lips and eyes swollen in the heat of ecstasy.

Inger from Sellanrå farm squats in the white hammock on Nørholm with her hand in the air. She has short, light hair and tattoos down her arm. Her index finger and pinkie form the sign for Satan's horns.

Fish balls wobble in their tin, making the brine flow over the edges and down the sides.

A sourdough bubbles, ferments, rises.

A carton of milk, skimmed, fortified with vitamin D, is opened and tipped over a glass.

A long wad of spit hangs from a pair of lips.

Thick blood spills from the skim-milk carton and covers the glass, which is actually upside-down, so the blood runs down the outside and over the table surface underneath, evenly.

A fountain of blood.

Raisins are sprinkled over a bowl of rice porridge, forming the image of labia, if that's what we want to think it looks like. Raspberry jam is added and the porridge grows redder and redder.

A six-year-old girl sucks her thumb with eyes closed.

Hands above the porridge, dripping milk and jam.

A Midgard serpent sucks its own tail energetically.

A banana that looks like the thumbs-up gesture is inserted into an inflatable vagina and disappears inside it.

Brown bread is sliced and blood comes out, as though it's a severed arm.

A group of witch girls in leather jackets, white T-shirts and jeans stage the Munch painting *The Day After* in the shed where Mayhem took some of their most famous press photos.

The three images are superimposed: the hungover lady from the Munch painting, Varg Vikernes from Mayhem and the witches.

A hand with rings and black nail polish with a silver shimmer picks up a white plastic knife and spreads a brown topping, maybe chocolate, maybe shit, on a slice of the brown bread.

The same hand stirs a bloody meat casserole with a wooden spoon, fast. Big bubbles and liquid shapes rise and fall in the pot, like animals that attempt to reach the surface but are stuck in the blood.

More fruits disappear into the same inflatable vagina. Plums, a green apple, a little pear. Grapes.

The thumb that's sucked starts bleeding.

Smoke rises from the spontaneously ignited occult fire of hatred.

A leech draws blood from a foot.

Gooseberries.

The hand with rings and nail polish stirs the meat casserole without a spoon, the whole hand stuck into it.

The witches that staged *The Day After* perform a version of *Puberty* in the same shed. One of them wears a nude suit and sits on the bench with arms held in a limp upside-down cross over the crotch. The other witches are covered in black body paint, and together they create the shadow behind the naked girl, against the graffitied wooden wall. One of them forms the girl's hair by sitting directly behind her and putting two black hands over her forehead while her elbows point down toward the shoulders on each side of the head. Then everyone looks up, peering at us with ferocious, seething eyes, hating.

Tinned sliced carrots.

The hand is stuck deeper and deeper into the boiling blood soup in the pot. It is reminiscent of a veterinarian's hand deep inside a cow's butt. As the arm is pulled out, it has a scruffy live chicken in its hand. The chicken squeaks.

Crabsticks.

Venke tears a sheet from *Pan*, third edition (1908, with gold typeface and a picture of clouds and sea in gold), puts page after page in her mouth and begins to chew. As her mouth fills with Hamsun's book, she thrusts her fingers in and tries to pack the brittle old paper tighter. Spit runs from both corners of her mouth and is also gold-coloured, like bright, thick urine.

Over this scene, Terese is reading a monologue: it might be audible, it's about the Apocalypse and its seven signs, first something about how the internet is drained, then about waffles contorting in their waffle irons, next about snowing streetscapes covered in white – it snows milk cartons, yoghurt cups, fish balls and grated white cheese – then she shouts that the goat's cheese will go rancid, and that the white and grey speckled wool sweaters will all simultaneously split their seams across the country, and the IKEA shelves, the IKEA chairs! Look! They're transformed into pick-up sticks and falling apart. We should never have chucked those Allen keys.

Then the skies fall, and techno and black metal, too. Lightning and thunderbolts strike across the country. Classroom set after classroom set of the New Testament fills with black ink. They rub out their own content, turning white to black. Soon The Old Testament follows; the chapters eat themselves and leave hundreds of pages of black monochrome, until Adam and Eve and the myth of creation and heaven are darkened and the earth is stuffed and backfilled.

Prawns.

Now the world prints a map of itself in 3D, in tones of blood.

Now the 3D printer prints two plastic people.

It's Terese and Venke, embracing each other like lovers hugging, or like newborn twins, or yin and yang. They suck each other's thumbs. They are smoking, they are hot, melting into each other until they resemble a puddle.

The chicken keeps squeaking.

Then the material gets colder, colder, cold.

The Pool

Look! We see Terese's and Venke's bodies fall, legs first, head and arms last. They are dressed in swimming costumes and fall in slow motion, so slowly that it's almost unbearable to watch. Centimetre by centimetre their feet come closer to the ground, which is shaped like a pool apparently filled with water. Since their movements are so drawn out, their bodies seem already stuck in something, something viscous, as if they are hanging in the air, as if we have opened a space between time once more, and the two are stuck in the mass between the milliseconds.

The beginnings of a shout can be heard in the distance, far inside the muscles deep down in the throat, extending into faint white noise that drones quietly in the stagnant room.

The two figures rush toward the surface in a long arc, making the skin on their faces, on their thighs and breasts and around their ankles, wobble infinitely slowly, like the heavy layers of stage curtains drawn up and down. Their skin is so elastic that it threatens to split and fall off, both upward and downward. In this infinity Venke and Terese look like unborn foetuses but also corpses, twisted by coagulated time, on their way to the underworld, the underwater world, the amniotic fluid world, down into the subculture.

Then we notice that the pool isn't filled with water, but with jelly, and that it isn't a pool, it's a cleverly made aspic shaped like a pool. Huge bits of prawn and peas the size of tennis balls are hidden in there. Eggs as big as rugby balls are scattered around, split in half or in quarters, but with red, not yellow, jelly yolks.

When Venke's and Terese's bodies finally hit the pool's surface, there is no splash, only a jiggle, and the gelatin swallows them both.

Aspic is a voyeuristic fantasy, a fantasy about being able to see through structures, through matter. We see straight through the form and into the contents. We see corpses in the ground, penis in vagina. The impenetrable web and enclosed surfaces that we're used to seeing on almost all other objects disappear with aspic. In the objects' place, the eye senses the possibility of hope, an alternative to the systems, an alternative that illuminates the mysterious and shows us what we ordinarily can't see. The aspic is like an X-ray; it stops what flows and opens up what is closed. The aspic gives us access to eternity.

The aspic, set in savoury gelatine, is in this way an invisible container, without air, gravity or time; it's 100 per cent texture. First concocted in the Middle Ages, it develops through centuries, parallel with the witch trials, reaching its peak in the 1950s. As the atom bombs and the hydrogen bombs are detonated and towns and landscapes and humans and animals are pulverised, thousands of cartons with aspic are congealing all over the world, and inside them are meticulously sliced fish morsels, seafood and vegetables.

When dinner is carried to the dining table later in the evening, it's the notion of creating a space for what's been blown to pieces that jiggles between the hands of the housewife. The soft but congealed world of the aspic dissolves gravity, and breeds absurd foetuses in its jellied, salty amniotic fluid, binding the chaos of the world as it quivers against the housewives' bodies. It's a draft of an alternative form of expression.

Aspic is made from the collagen in the bone marrow of pigs, and I dream it's also made from our own bones and our own marrow, because marrow is the very best we have to give of ourselves. In the marrow is found the collagen, the creative power, the coherence. The same sounds ring in *marrow* as in *margin*. In my language it's even the same word. In the margins are the experiments, the bonus material, the unwritten scenes, the unused leftovers, a suggestion for a new world, a suggestion for impossible connections. In the margins are the comments, the hope and hate, suspended in the thick, translucent marrow broth.

Aspic is the original internet.

Aspic teaches me to write.

Aspic is our own man-made blasphemy.

I send Venke and Terese into the aspic. They're lying there, fixed, perhaps with their heads poking above the surface, like two earrings fastened to the soft cloth lining of a gift box.

Below their heads I see chopped up bits of animals and plants, and now also Venke and Terese, liberated from their original form, components stirred together in random monstrous combinations. The aspic becomes a place for the impossible. In that place God can't see us, I think, because there's no I left. We escape our sinful subjects: I'm not a subject, but subversive.

Maybe this is what we call 'magic'. Maybe this is 'darkness'. Maybe this is the magical place where we can find each other. Maybe this is where I can get closer to you.

As I lie like an egg yolk, eyes shut in the thick mass, I feel you out there somewhere, in the same mass. Maybe this kind of love is the root of all witchcraft, to reshape dimensions to get closer to each other; maybe by writing this, I can bind us together.

and?

Tell me,
    did we ever get that close?